AF508012

The Vampire Priest
By Jonathan Gleich

MESSAGE FROM THE AUTHOR:

Twenty years ago, I visited my sister in England. We drove past a church on Romney Marsh. That moment inspired this story.

This isn't the usual vampire story. No fangs in moonlight. No sex. What you'll find instead: a vampire priest, a sanctuary for the lost and the abandoned, and a story that asks *why* vampires work the way they do—and actually answers it.

If that sounds like your kind of story, welcome. If not, no hard feelings.

ACKNOWLEDGMENTS

I would like to thank Terri Rioux for being the beta reader of this story and providing excellent feedback.

DEDICATION

This book is dedicated to Linda Cappel, who was the first person to encourage me to write. It only took twenty years...

***

Find out more about the story and the author at vampirepriest.com

THE VAMPIRE PRIEST
By Jonathan Gleich
Paperback Edition

Chapter I -- The Sermon

Thursday:

The last of the congregation had gone perhaps twenty minutes ago, their voices fading across the causeway, swallowed by the marsh. Gregory had stood at the door and watched them go the way he always did -- until the last car disappeared and the only sounds were the watercourses and the sheep and the particular silence that Romney Marsh made when it had the evening to itself.

He ducked back inside.

The door of St Thomas à Becket required it. Always had. People were smaller when it was built. Gregory was not. Every person who entered this church bowed their head, whether they intended to or not -- the ancient timber frame made no allowances for the modern human frame, and Gregory had long since stopped noticing the motion. He simply ducked. The way you breathe. The way you put the kettle on.

Inside, the church surprised people. It always did. The exterior offered nothing -- plain brick, heavy red tiles gone dark with age and lichen, a squat tower that made no grand claims about itself. But inside, there were the white pews. They stood in their painted rows, bright and improbable, the kind of white that had no business surviving six centuries of damp Kent winters. The triple-decker pulpit rose above them like something from a theatre -- which, Gregory had always thought, was not entirely wrong.

One of the parishioners, Abigail, had left a pie on the counter by the stove, covered with a clean cloth. Apple and cinnamon, still warm, the smell of it reaching all the way into the nave. She did this occasionally, without announcement, without expecting thanks. It was simply there when he came back through.

He would have it after tea.

The candles were burning down. He moved through the pews, checking them, his hand trailing along the smooth wood. He knew this building the way he knew his own hands -- the cold spot near the north wall that no amount of heating had ever addressed, the third flagstone from the door that rocked slightly if you stepped on the left edge, the particular drawer in the vestry that required lifting before pulling. He had been here eleven years. The church had been here since 1200. They had reached an accommodation.

Through the small windows, the marsh was going golden. The watercourses caught the last of the light. Somewhere outside, sheep were making their opinions known about something. The causeway stretched away toward the road, empty now, the evening settling over the flat Kent landscape with the unhurried certainty of something that had been doing this for a very long time.

He was smiling to himself. The sermon had gone well.

Gregory Chadwick knew this the way he always knew -- not from the faces in the pews, though those had been good too, attentive in the particular way that meant something had landed rather than merely been heard. He knew it from the quality of the silence afterwards. The way the congregation filed out. The handshakes that lasted a fraction longer than usual -- the clasps on his shoulders, the smiles. Margaret had nodded, which from Margaret meant everything.

This week's sermon had been on circles. The circle of life. Not the song -- he had made that joke himself before anyone else could, which was the only way to survive making it. Like ripples on still water, he had said. Each one is its own. Each one changes everything it touches.

He had been pleased with it.

He still was.

He was reaching for his cup when the door opened.

He did not hear a knock. There was never a knock. The door of St Thomas à Becket was not the kind of door people knocked on. It was the kind of door that was simply -- open. Had always been open. Gregory had never once considered locking it and did not intend to start.

He turned.

The man in the doorway was not old. Gregory registered this first, and then immediately understood that it was wrong, that old was entirely the wrong word, that this man was something the English language had not quite got around to naming properly. He was not old. He was ancient. There was a difference that Gregory felt in his chest before his mind caught up with it. He looked thirty-five, perhaps. But his eyes were older. Much, much older.

He was tall He ducked through the low door and straightened up slowly, the way a man does when straightening up has become a considered act. There was something military in the way he stood -- not modern military, but older. Pale in a way that had nothing to do with illness -- a pallor that looked permanent, geological, as though it had always been there. His face was mapped with red lines and the particular texture of skin worn by time. His collar sat oddly. Too high. As though there was something beneath it.

He was carrying the world's history on his shoulders.

Too much drink, Gregory thought.

And moved toward the man. Because that was what he did.

"Come in," Gregory said, which was unnecessary since the man was already in, but the words filled the space between them, and that was what words were for.

"Please, sit."

The man looked at him. His eyes were the colour of ash -- not brown, not grey. Something that had been a colour once and forgotten how.

He sat. His name, he said, was Edmund.

He did not offer a surname. Gregory did not ask for one.

They chatted for perhaps fifteen minutes. Perhaps twenty. Gregory would not be entirely certain afterwards, because the conversation had the quality of something outside ordinary time -- not dramatic, not urgent, just unusually still. The man called Edmund listened. Completely. Without waiting for his turn.

"My life has been circles," Edmund said. "You drop a pebble in the water, and the circles multiply. I touch one person, that person touches three, those three touch ten. Soon, hundreds, thousands are affected by a single touch. It is all a simple matter of time."

Gregory considered this.

"I do something similar," he said. "With the word of God. You hope that the people you touch reach out to others. Share what they've been given."

Edmund looked at him.

"Yes," he said quietly. "Exactly that."

Gregory offered him tea.

Edmund smiled. It was a good smile. It had been practised for a very long time.

"It would ruin my appetite," he said.

Gregory nodded and moved about the small kitchen area at the back of the church, the familiar geography of it, the particular drawer that stuck, the mug with the chip on the handle he kept meaning to throw away. Behind him, the conversation continued. Edmund was asking questions about the sermon that were more specific than they should have been. More precise. The kind of questions that came from someone who had thought about circles for a very long time.

"I was listening," Edmund said. "Before I came in. I heard the words. Saw the lights. Felt the heartbeats. All inside."

He paused.

"It touched me, and drew me in."

Gregory turned slightly, interested. This was not an unusual thing to say, precisely, but the way he said it -- the particular weight on the word heartbeats -- was unusual. He filed it away. He was good at filing things away.

"I'm glad," Gregory said. And meant it.

He was filling the kettle with water when Edmund spoke again.

"I admire you," Edmund said. "Your sermon convinced me of that. And you are not afraid of death -- you spoke about that as well."

Gregory paused at the kettle.

"Most men wear the fear of death like an overcoat," Edmund continued. "One they never remove. It sits with them at meals. Walks beside them in the street. Always present. Always waiting."

He watched Gregory.

"Yours is not there."

Gregory thought about it. He always thought about things before he answered. It was one of the things his bishop found annoying, and his congregation found steadying.

"I am a man of God," Gregory said. "If death is how I meet him, then it was the way God intended." He paused. "Do I fear death? No. Do I fear the next step? Of course." Another pause. "But if I do leave this world, I leave it better."

Edmund was very still.

"I learned something today," he said. "I spent so much time learning. I never thought there was anything more to learn."

Edmund suddenly stood.

Gregory lit the flame under the kettle.

"I should have stayed outside," Edmund said.

Suddenly, he was by Gregory's side. His hand on Gregory's shoulder -- firm, not forceful. Almost brotherly. Affectionate.

Edmund gently turned Gregory toward him. His hand moved to Gregory's jaw, tilting his head. He pressed his face to Gregory's neck with the quiet certainty of something that has done this a thousand times. And fed.

The air felt heavy. Still. Even the candles didn't flicker.

It may have been moments. It may have been hours. The two men stood there in that strange embrace whilst the marsh outside went fully dark and the sheep fell silent, and the watercourses ran on without caring.

The kettle began to whistle. Softly at first. The ordinary world, insisting on itself.

Gregory didn't know how long he had been somewhere else. The pain was there -- considerable, and wrong -- and the grunting that filled his ears was Edmund's, not his. Low. Rhythmic. Edmund had gone somewhere else entirely.

The whistle cut through it. Small and persistent and utterly indifferent to what was happening in this church tonight.

It brought him back.

A verse arrived in his head. Not summoned. Just -- there.

His hand found the cross. Heavy. Dark with age. One edge worn sharper by time. A thing he had carried so long it had become part of the geography of his body.

The man's ear was very close to his face. Edmund's hair smelled of peat and cold places and something Gregory could not name. And the church was still there around him -- the candles still burning, the box pews in their painted white rows.

The kettle whistled.

Gregory's hand found the cross. Pulled it free.

He drove it into Edmund's chest.

Edmund stepped back.

He looked down at the cross, then up at Gregory.

Gregory realised he was a vampire.

"You are nothing more than a mosquito," Gregory said.

Edmund blinked.

"What --"

"And I am just your next meal."

As the cross sank into Edmund's chest, he looked up at Gregory.

His face shifted -- shock, then sudden delight.

"Thank you," Edmund said.

His body turned to dust and fell to the ground.

The thunderclap came out of nowhere.

Romney Marsh in spring was not without weather, but this was not weather. This was a single sound, clean and total -- the kind of thing that makes animals stop and look up. It rolled across the marsh and was gone.

In the silence that followed, where Sir Edmund of Warwick had been standing, there was dust. Just dust. Settling on the flagstone floor of a church that had been standing since 1200, that had weathered plague and reformation and two world wars and the steady managed decline of English Christianity, that had been cold in January and slightly damp in March and full of sheep smells in October, that had been many things to many people across many centuries.

The dust settled into the crevices -- as if the church were welcoming it. Giving it a place to rest.

It was still standing.

Gregory stood in it. His breathing was returning to something like normal.

He touched his neck. His hand came away wet. There would be something in the vestry cupboard -- there always was. He had stitched his own hand twice in this church. He could manage a bleeding neck.

He found the cupboard. Antiseptic. A bandage left over from when Ted had caught his hand on the gate latch three winters ago. He worked carefully, methodically, in the small mirror above the basin.

Something glinted on the floor. He crouched. Picked it up.

A fragment of chain mail. Small. Almost like a necklace, worn smooth, old in a way he could feel rather than date. Old in the way the church was old -- not ancient as an object, but ancient as a presence. Something that had been somewhere for a very long time. He turned it over in his hands.

He did not know what it was yet. Not really. He had ideas about what it might be, and he set them aside carefully, the way he set all unconfirmed things aside, in the part of his mind marked to be returned to.

He put it in his pocket.

The kettle had continued its soft whistle.

Gregory looked at the dust on the flagstones. At the cross in his hand. At the space where a man had been.

He was, he realised, quite hungry. He had not eaten since lunch.

He went and made his tea.

Margaret came by the following morning, the way she always came by -- with purpose and without announcement. She saw the pie on the counter, untouched under its cloth. She tutted. She saw the small dark stain on the flagstone near the door and tutted again. Clumsy oaf.

She had heard the thunderclap the night before. Storm coming in off the marsh, she had thought.

Wind must have caught the door.

The dust was intolerable. She found the broom.

She put the pie in the fridge.

She put the kettle on.

***

Chapter II -- The Physician

Friday:

The first thing Gregory noticed the morning after was the jar.

It had been stuck on the kitchen shelf for the better part of a month. Strawberry preserve. He had tried it twice, concluded it had been over-tightened at the factory, and left it for Ted, who had better hands for that sort of thing. On Friday morning, he picked it up without thinking, and it opened.

He stood there for a moment looking at the lid.

He made his toast. He filed the jar away in the part of his mind marked to be returned to and went about his morning.

The wound on his neck had stopped hurting. This was the second thing, and harder to file away, because wounds did not simply stop after a day. They hurt, then hurt less, and eventually ceased altogether, following rules Gregory understood. This pain had simply vanished. What remained was something else: a small, steady pulse beneath the skin, patient and insistent, entirely separate from the one in his chest.

He checked the stitches in the vestry mirror on Friday morning and found them redundant. The wound had closed. The skin beneath, when he carefully removed them, was smooth but still bruised with two purple circles. He dropped the stitches in the bin and stood for a moment looking at his own reflection.

The man looking back at him appeared entirely ordinary.

This was either reassuring or the opposite. He had not yet decided which.

***

The hunger started on Saturday and got more intense.

It was not the ordinary hunger of a missed meal or a busy morning. It was something more fundamental -- his body had developed opinions about what it required and was making them known with unusual persistence. He found himself at the butchers in the village on Saturday afternoon buying pork and black pudding, which he did not ordinarily eat much of, and standing in front of the haggis for rather longer than was necessary before deciding that haggis on a Saturday afternoon felt excessive, even given the circumstances.

He ate the black pudding for dinner. He ate it again for Sunday breakfast. It was, he had to admit, very, very good.

***

He reached for the sugar in his tea on Sunday morning, took one sip, and put the mug down. Wrong. Processed. Something underneath the sweetness that his tongue had abruptly decided it did not want. He made a fresh cup and found the honey at the back of the cupboard. That was considerably better. He stood at the kitchen window drinking it and watching the marsh , thinking about nothing in particular, which was not something he was usually able to do.

He delivered the morning service. Nobody noticed anything different. He noticed that he could smell the cold coming off Mrs. Alderton's coat from three pews away, and that the robin had built a nest under the north eave, and that Ted had eaten something with a great deal of onion at some point before arriving. He filed all of this away.

A pen rolled off the pulpit. His left hand caught it without him breaking stride.

He slept deeply that night. He dreamed of flying -- not the anxious, falling-upward kind, but something purposeful and clear, as though he had somewhere to be and knew exactly how to get there. He woke with the sense of having been somewhere and done something that had made considerable sense at the time.

He made an appointment with the doctor, for Monday morning.

He did not mention any of this to anyone. There was no one to mention it to, and besides, he had not yet decided what it was.

***

Monday:

The waiting room of Dr. Patel's surgery held four chairs, a small table, a leaflet about the importance of fibre in the diet, a leaflet about managing stress, and a magazine from six months ago containing an article about how to swing a golf club like a professional. Gregory read all of it. He was not a golfer and had no intention of becoming one, but the waiting room was warm and quiet, and reading about grip pressure kept his mind from going places he wasn't ready for it to go.

The sensation in his neck continued. He noticed it more in stillness -- the throb that was not his pulse, patient and separate, carrying on its business without consulting him.

He picked up the fibre leaflet again.

***

Dr. Patel was a small man with large glasses and the manner of someone who had heard everything and was therefore surprised by nothing. He had been Gregory's physician for nine years and a parishioner of St Thomas à Becket for seven of those. They had an understanding.

"Sit down, Father Chadwick," he said, not looking up. "What seems to be the trouble?"

"I was bitten," Gregory said, without emotion. "Three days ago. On the neck."

Dr. Patel looked up.

"Bitten."

"By what animal?" Dr. Patel said.

"By a man."

Dr. Patel removed his glasses, polished them, and replaced them. Gregory recognised this as thinking time.

"And this man -- was this an altercation of some kind? An angry Protestant, perhaps? A difference of theological opinion?" He attempted a small jest.

"Nothing of the sort," Gregory said, and smiled.

"Have you reported it?"

"I have not."

Dr. Patel made a note. Gregory did not try to read it.

"May I look at the wound?"

Gregory turned his head. Dr. Patel examined the neck with a small torch and the focused attention he brought to everything.

"Two puncture wounds," he said. "Significant bruising. -- " A pause. " -- the healing is quite remarkable. For three days."

"Yes."

"The location and spacing suggest canines. Cuspids." He straightened. "Whoever bit you had considerably enlarged cuspids. Unusually so."

"I rather thought that might be the case."

Dr. Patel looked at him steadily.

"Some studies suggest certain tooth development genes -- potentially inherited from the Neanderthal lineage -- can be found in people of European descent. It is not unheard of."

"Of course," Gregory said.

"Were you bitten by a bat at any point? A pipistrelle, greater horseshoe, long-eared? I am sure there are bats living in the church -- I am simply eliminating possibilities."

"No. A man."

"You're quite certain."

"Reasonably," Gregory said. "Yes."

"Where is this man now?"

"He disappeared," Gregory said.

"Let's talk about the symptoms." Dr, Patel asked, Gregory listed them in the order they had presented themselves: the accelerated healing, the hunger and its specific character, the black pudding, and the honey. He mentioned the jar of strawberry preserve. He mentioned the pew cushions he had carried in one armload on Sunday when he normally did two trips. He mentioned the pen. He mentioned the flying dreams. He mentioned the heartbeat in his neck.

Dr. Patel wrote steadily throughout.

"Increased iron craving following blood loss is not uncommon," he said.

"The haggis?"

"That is somewhat more specific."

"The honey -- I switched from sugar. The sugar tasted wrong."

"You may have developed a sensitivity. To the lime or massecuite used in processing."

"Ah. Yes. That would explain it."

"The flying dreams are not uncommon following trauma. The mind processes significant events in sleep."

"Quite."

"The strength and the healing rate are more interesting."

He set down his pen. He looked at Gregory over his glasses with the expression of a man choosing to honour nine years of accumulated professional respect.

"I would like to do a full blood panel," Dr. Patel said. "Given what I'm seeing with the healing rate -- I want to be thorough. Make sure there is no infection present."

Gregory held out his arm without being asked. Dr. Patel found the vein. Gregory looked at the ceiling.

Dr. Patel noticed. Gregory smiled. "Can't stand the sight of blood," he said.

Dr. Patel said nothing. He made a note.

***

Tuesday

Dr. Patel said. He would ring him up.

> *He did not ring.*

He appeared at the church on Tuesday morning. He had not come on a Tuesday since his wife's mother had died three years ago, and he had needed somewhere quiet to sit.

Gregory made tea. Dr. Patel sat in one of the white box pews, held his cup with both hands, and looked at it.

"The results," he said finally, "are unusual."

"How unusual?"

"I've sent them to a colleague in London. Dr. Sarah Okonkwo. She specialises in uncommon haematological presentations."

Gregory nodded.

"I have been practising medicine for twenty-three years," Dr. Patel said. Still looking at his tea.

"I know."

"In that time, I have seen a great many things."

"I imagine so."

"What I cannot account for -- using any framework currently available to me -- is what your blood appears to be doing."

Gregory waited.

"Your Erythrocytosis levels are elevated across the spectrum -- as though your cells are being deprived of oxygen. But you do not smoke, and there is no physiological reason for it. Your Leukocytosis levels are almost double the norm. Typically, that indicates infection, inflammation, or an immune system disorder. And your blood protein count -- Hyperproteinemia -- is extremely high."

He paused.

"It appears," Dr. Patel said, "to be changing."

They sat with that. The marsh light came through the small windows. Outside, a sheep made a considered remark about something.

"I see," Gregory said.

"Dr. Okonkwo will want to see you. I have already made the appointment. Wednesday."

Gregory had a confirmation class on Wednesday afternoon. He could move it. He would ring Mrs. Hartley. She would be disappointed, but she would manage.

"Gregory," Dr. Patel said. First time in nine years. "Are you all right?"

Gregory thought about it properly. "I don't know yet," he said. "But I expect I shall be."

Dr. Patel nodded once, the way he filed things. "The referral letter," he said, "will be somewhat challenging to write."

"I imagine it will."

"I shall do my best."

"You always do," Gregory said.

"I am writing you a script for antibiotics, as well as an iron supplement. Fill them with the chemists and start taking them immediately."

Dr. Patel finished his tea. Put on his coat. Walked to the door, ducked through it without being reminded, and crossed the causeway without looking back.

Gregory sat alone in the white box pews.

His neck throbbed. Steady. Patient. A heartbeat that was not quite his.

He thought about Sunday's sermon. About Mrs. Hartley. About the jar of strawberry preserve, he had opened it without trying.

He thought about the thing Dr. Patel had not quite said.

He put the kettle on.

***

Chapter III -- The Pilgrimage

Gregory found Ted in the churchyard on Tuesday afternoon, trimming the grass along the east wall with the focused attention of a man who considers tidiness a form of prayer.

"Ted," he said. "Could you drive me to London on Wednesday morning? I have a doctor's appointment."

Ted straightened up. He considered this the way he considered most things -- briefly, thoroughly, and without making a performance of it.

"Of course, Father. While I'm in town, I can do some shopping for the missus."

"It's a two-hour drive," Gregory said.

"Or I could drive you to Rye, and you could take the Marshlink. Be a shorter trip for you."

Gregory thought about this. The train would mean sitting with strangers. The car would mean sitting with Ted, who would not ask questions.

"The car would be good," Gregory said. "If you're certain."

"Seven o'clock?"

"Seven o'clock," Gregory agreed.

Ted returned to the grass. Gregory went back inside. Neither of them mentioned it again until Wednesday morning.

Ted's car was a ten-year-old Volvo that smelled of dog and WD-40 and something Gregory had always assumed was the particular scent of reliability. It was very clean. It had never once broken down in Gregory's experience, which he suspected was less to do with luck than with Ted's habit of attending to things before they became problems.

They left the marsh as the light was coming up. The causeway in the early morning, the watercourses silver on either side, the sheep still and indifferent. Then the road north through the flatlands, and gradually the world filling in around them -- other cars, other roads, the landscape becoming more managed and less ancient as they moved away from Romney Marsh and toward the motorway.

Ted drove the way he did everything. Steadily. Without drama.

Gregory watched England go past and thought about Dr. Okonkwo.

He thought about the jar. The stitches. The pen catching itself in his left hand. He thought about the hunger, which had not diminished, and the heartbeat in his neck, which had not stopped, and the flying dreams, which continued with the consistency of something that had decided to stay.

He thought about what Dr. Patel had not quite said.

It appears to be changing.

He had been a man of God for eleven years. Before that, a man who intended to become one. He was accustomed to sitting with uncertainty. It was, in many ways, the central skill of the vocation -- the ability to hold questions open, to resist the comfort of false resolution, to wait with something you did not yet understand.

He was waiting now. He was quite good at it.

"You all right, Father?" Ted said, somewhere on the M20.

"Quite well," Gregory said. "Thank you."

Ted nodded. They did not speak again until London.

***

Ted dropped him outside 108 Harley Street with the businesslike efficiency of someone who had delivered things to difficult places before and intended to collect them again in good order.

"I'll be back at two," Ted said.

"I may not be that long." --

"I'll be back at two," Ted said again, which Gregory understood to mean that the shopping for the missus would take until two and that this was simply the arrangement.

"Thank you, Ted."

Ted drove away. Gregory turned to face the building.

Harley Street at nine in the morning was its own particular world -- a procession of people carrying the careful expressions of those who had been told something, or were about to be told something, and were managing the information with varying degrees of success. Gregory felt entirely at home in it. He had sat with people in exactly this condition for eleven years.

He went inside.

***

Dr. Sarah Okonkwo was not what Gregory had expected, though he would have been hard-pressed to say what he had expected. She was tall, precise in her movements, with the focused quality of someone whose attention, when directed at you, felt like being properly seen. She had Dr. Patel's results open on her screen when he came in and did not look up immediately, which Gregory found he did not mind. It suggested the results were worth looking at.

"Father Chadwick," she said finally, and looked up. "Please sit down."

He sat.

She studied him for a moment with the frank assessment of someone whose profession required it.

"Dr. Patel has given me a thorough account," she said. "I have some questions of my own. But first -- how are you feeling?"

"Hungry," Gregory said. "Mostly."

Something shifted in her expression. Not an alarm. Interest.

"What are you craving?"

"Meat. Pork particularly. Black pudding. I've been eating a great deal of black pudding."

"And you've switched from sugar to honey."

"Yes."

She made a note. Looked back at the screen.

"The healing rate is extraordinary," she said. "Dr. Patel is not given to hyperbole. If he says the wound closed in twenty-four hours, I believe him."

"It may have been faster than that," Gregory said.

She looked at him.

"How much faster?"

"I'm not certain. I noticed it was closed on Friday morning. It happened Thursday night."

She made another note. Her pen moved quickly and without pause, which Gregory found reassuring. It suggested she was finding categories for things.

"May I examine you?"

"Of course."

She came around the desk with the unhurried efficiency of someone who had done this ten thousand times. She examined the wound site with a small torch and gloved hands, turning his head gently, pressing lightly around the edges of the healed punctures.

"Remarkable," she said quietly. Not to him. To herself.

She checked his blood pressure. Noted something. Checked it again.

"Your blood pressure is elevated," she said. "Significantly. Are you aware of that?"

"I am not," Gregory said.

"How is your sleep?"

"Deep. Very deep. I dream."

"The flying dreams Dr. Patel mentioned."

"Yes."

"Every night?"

"Every night since Thursday."

She returned to her desk. She looked at the results for a long moment before she spoke again.

"In reading Dr. Patel's report, I see a correlation with your diet," she said. "The foods you're gravitating toward are all blood-based, iron-rich."

She glanced at the results.

"Your oxygen saturation is extremely low. Most people sit between ninety-two and one hundred."

Gregory said nothing.

"In cases of chronic hypoxemia, the body compensates. It produces more red blood cells -- erythrocytosis. It attempts to carry more oxygen."

A pause.

"What is unusual is the degree. Is the speed."

She looked at him again.

"Your body appears to be demanding iron to support this process."

Gregory nodded. This was, he thought, a remarkably orderly explanation for something that had not felt orderly at all.

"I would like to put you on additional nutrition to work in harmony with your current diet," she said. "There are blood-derived protein supplements. Porcine-based. Developed for medical use."

She made a note.

"I can source them."

A glance at the results.

"If we proceed, Dr. Patel will need to run weekly panels. Full blood work. We'll monitor your iron levels closely."

A small pause.

"If this is driving the erythrocytosis, excess iron becomes a risk. Haemochromatosis. Toxicity. We would need to stay ahead of it."

"In the interim," she said, "we may need to supplement further."

A brief pause.

"Bovine blood is used in certain medical and nutritional contexts. Combined with a protein base, it would provide a controlled source of iron."

She did not look away from the results.

"It is not a long-term solution."

Another pause.

"But it may stabilise you whilst we determine what this is." "I imagine it will taste unpleasant," she said, with a small smile. "The most effective treatments often are."

Gregory looked at her.

"I'm a priest," he said. "I'm no stranger to unpleasant things being necessary."

She almost smiled at that. Almost.

She asked him about the bite itself. He gave her the same account he had given Dr. Patel -- a man, an altercation, the neck, six days ago. She listened without interrupting. When he finished, she was quiet for a moment.

"The wound site," she said carefully. "Is there any sensation there now?"

"A throb," Gregory said. "Not pain. More like -- " He considered. " -- a second heartbeat. Separate from my own."

She wrote that down. Underlined it. Did not explain why.

"I would like to take my own samples," she said. "Today. A full panel -- every conceivable test. I want a complete picture."

"Of course."

"I should warn you -- I will be taking eight vials of blood. You may feel light-headed for several hours afterwards."

Gregory considered this.

"That seems appropriate," he said. "Given the circumstances."

She looked at him for a moment that was slightly longer than strictly clinical.

"I will be in touch with Dr. Patel. He'll arrange the weekly panels."

"Father Chadwick." She paused. "What you are experiencing is unusual. I want to be honest with you about that. I have seen presentations that resemble elements of this. I have not seen this precisely."

Gregory nodded.

"I don't expect you to have seen this precisely," he said. "Neither have I."

"Two weeks," she said. "And ring if anything changes."

"I will."

She pressed a button on her desk. A moment later, her nurse appeared at the door.

"Mr. Chadwick will need a full panel," Dr. Okonkwo said. "Eight vials. Please make him comfortable."

The nurse -- a compact, efficient woman who reminded Gregory somewhat of Margaret -- nodded and held the door open.

Gregory followed her down the corridor.

He sat in a small room with a reclining chair and a framed print of the Norfolk Broads on the wall and held very still whilst eight vials were filled from his arm, one after another, each one labelled with a speed and precision that suggested this was the least unusual part of anyone's Wednesday morning.

He looked at the ceiling.

He thought about the sermon for next Sunday.

He thought about haemochromatosis and what it would mean if his iron levels became toxic, which they apparently might, and filed that away in the part of his mind marked to be returned to.

"All done," the nurse said. "Take your time getting up."

He thanked her. He stood carefully. He did feel slightly light-headed, which he thought was only fair.

He went back out into Harley Street and stood on the pavement in the Wednesday morning air and thought about bovine blood and the particular expression on Dr. Okonkwo's face when she had underlined the words second heartbeat.

His neck throbbed. Patient as ever. He found a bench. He sat down. He thought about nothing for a while, which he was getting rather better at.

At two o'clock precisely, Ted's Volvo appeared at the end of the street.

"How did it go?" Ted said when Gregory got in.

"Well enough," Gregory said. "She was very thorough."

Ted nodded. He pulled out into the traffic.

"Get the shopping done?" Gregory asked.

"Most of it. Couldn't find the particular thing she wanted. I'll try elsewhere."

They drove in comfortable silence through the city and out onto the motorway. Gregory watched London give way to the home counties and then to Kent, the landscape flattening and opening as they went south, the sky getting bigger.

Romney Marsh came back to meet them -- the watercourses, the sheep, the causeway, the church standing in its field as though it had not moved in eight hundred years.

Because it hadn't.

"Ted," Gregory said, as they crossed the causeway.

"Father."

"Thank you. For today."

"If this turns into a regular London trip," Gregory said, "I can take the train. You'd just need to drive me to Rye."

Ted was quiet for a moment.

"We'll discuss it once we have a clearer idea," he said.

He parked the car. He turned off the engine. Gregory sat for a moment in the passenger seat of the Volvo that smelled of dog and WD-40, looking at the church.

"Same time next fortnight," Ted said.

"How did you know?"

"Two weeks is standard for a follow-up," Ted said. "When they're not sure what they're looking at."

He got out. Gregory sat a moment longer. Same time next fortnight.

He got out. He ducked through the low door. He put the kettle on.

***

Chapter IV -- The Communion

He was reading from Corinthians when the smell distracted him.

Burning plastic. Sweet underneath, with rough edges. Not unpleasant exactly, more like something that had no business being in a church on a Sunday morning.

He lost his place.

Or do you not know that your body is the temple of the Holy Spirit who is in you...

He found it again. Carried on. But his attention had gone somewhere else, scanning the pews the way he now scanned them, reading the room in ways he had not been able to three weeks ago. Mrs. Alderton's lavender. Ted's soap. The cold coming off the flagstones.

And this. Burning plastic. Sweet and wrong.

He found it in the third pew on the left. Morris Phillips, sitting in his usual spot, large and good-natured, his coat slightly too small across the shoulders. Morris had been coming to St Thomas à Becket long before Gregory had arrived. A farmer, he brought vegetable baskets to families who needed them. He always smelled of cigarettes.

Today, he smelled of something else.

Gregory finished the reading. He delivered the sermon. He administered communion with the same careful attention he always gave it, moving through the familiar motions whilst the burning plastic smell settled at the back of his mind and stayed there.

After the service, when the church had emptied to its particular post-Sunday quiet, he found Morris still in his pew, coat buttoned, with no apparent rush to leave.

"Morris," Gregory said, and sat down beside him. "How are you keeping?"

Morris smiled. His teeth were the colour of caramel corn. "Funny you should ask, Father. I was just diagnosed with lung cancer. Start treatment in a fortnight. I was reflecting on it."

Gregory said nothing for a moment. Not because he was surprised -- the smell had told him something was wrong before Morris had said a word, but because some moments deserved a breath before you filled them.

"I'll pray for you," he said. "And I'll add your name to the intercessions. If you or your family need transport to the hospital, to appointments, the church car is available. You only need to ask."

Morris thanked him for the prayers and the offer, both.

He said his daughter was managing the driving for now, but he'd keep it in mind.

Gregory walked him to the door. He watched him cross the causeway, slower than he used to be.

He stood in the doorway for a moment after Morris had gone, the marsh stretching flat and silver around the church, and thought about temples of the Holy Spirit and what it meant when the temple needed tending.

Then he went inside and was immediately, violently sick.

He had made porridge. This had seemed like a reasonable thing to do -- he had been eating relatively normally for three days, if one counted black pudding and honey as normal, and porridge was plain and gentle and the sort of thing a body recovering from something ought to manage.

His body had a different view.

He stood at the kitchen sink for rather a long time afterwards, looking out at the marsh, feeling entirely hollow and considering the situation.

He tried the tea with honey. That came up too.

He tried a small spoonful of black pudding. That stayed down. His stomach made noises that would have frightened Satan. He waited. It stayed down.

He picked up the phone and rang Dr. Okonkwo. He left a message on her voicemail.

She rang back within twenty minutes.

"Father Chadwick."

"Please," he said. "Call me Gregory."

A pause. "Gregory." She said it as though testing whether it fit. Then said it again, more settled. "Gregory. What's happened?"

He told her about the porridge. The tea. The black pudding staying down.

"I was afraid this might develop," she said. "Your digestive system is adapting. The liver, the pancreas, and the gallbladder -- they process nutrients through bile and enzymes. Those systems are changing. Your body is learning to prioritise one thing."

"Blood," Gregory said.

"Yes. Solid food is becoming increasingly difficult to process. What your body needs has to be delivered in its simplest form."

A pause.

"Do you have any raw meat in the refrigerator? Packaged -- with blood visible?"

"Please hold on," Gregory said.

He set the phone on the counter and opened the fridge. Margaret had left a package of meat for a roast. He could see the blood collecting at one corner of the packaging -- at least quarter litre. He picked it up and came back to the phone.

"Yes. Margaret left a joint. There's blood in the packaging."

"I want you to poke a hole in the container," Dr. Okonkwo said, "and drain the blood into a cup. Then I want you to sip it and tell me how your body reacts."

Gregory looked at the package. He looked at the cup on the draining board -- bone china, white, part of the set Margaret had given him three Christmases ago.

"Right," he said. "Please stand by."

He did as he was told. The blood was dark and cold, and he found himself holding the cup at arm's length, as though it might do something unpredictable. He had always been squeamish at the sight of blood and avoided it whenever it was possible, but this was different. This was intentional. This was a choice.

He closed his eyes. He took a sip.

He opened his eyes.

Cold. A shiver at the temperature. Salt and metal and something underneath that he did not immediately have a word for. Not pleasant, exactly. Not unpleasant. He took another sip and waited.

He picked up the phone.

"That was unusual," he said. "It stayed down. It was almost pleasant. Metallic."

The nausea was gone. Completely. And he was, he realised, still holding the cup, and he wanted more of what was in it, and he set it down on the counter with some care and stood very still for a moment.

He did not mention that last part.

Dr. Okonkwo sounded relieved. "That confirms the hypothesis. The infection is prioritising your system to process blood. The changes are accelerating."

"What about trichinosis?" Gregory said. "Any risk?"

"Trichinella larvae inhabit the meat itself, not the blood. And this is a temporary measure until I can see you. Can you come to London today?"

"I'll ring Ted," Gregory said.

Ted was available.

Of course, Ted was available. Gregory had not yet determined whether Ted was simply a man with a flexible schedule or a man who understood that being available was a form of ministry in itself. He suspected the latter but had never asked.

They left the marsh at nine. The same route as before -- the causeway, the flatlands, the motorway filling in around them. Ted drove. Gregory looked out the window and thought about the cup on the kitchen counter and the fact that he had wanted to finish it.

He thought about that for quite a long time.

Ted said nothing until the M20.

"All right, Father?"

"I'm not sure, Ted. I'm not sure," Gregory said.

Ted nodded.

Chapter V -- The Redemption

"In him we have redemption through his blood, the forgiveness of our trespasses, according to the riches of his grace." -- Ephesians 1:7

Traffic was lighter on a Sunday morning. They were in London by quarter past ten.

There were fewer people on the streets than on a weekday, mostly tourists in bright colours, chatting and photographing things. Gregory squinted. The colours were doing something uncomfortable to his eyes, the light bouncing off the pavement in a way that felt invasive.

Ted reached up to his visor without being asked and handed Gregory a pair of sunglasses.

"Try these."

"Much better. Thank you, Ted."

Ted parked in a car park across the street from 108 Harley Street. They walked together to the door.

"Mind if I escort you today?" Ted said as they reached the entrance.

Flat. No particular inflection.

"It will be mind-numbingly dull," Gregory said. "But of course."

Dr. Okonkwo was waiting for them at her office door, which Gregory noted with some surprise. She was wearing street clothes -- trousers, a T-shirt, a waistcoat -- and looked dressed for something considerably more relaxed than a medical consultation. She opened the door as they approached.

"I've been expecting you."

"Dr. Okonkwo," Gregory said. "It's my pleasure to introduce Ted. My churchwarden. And driver."

Ted tipped his hat. "Pleasure to make your acquaintance."

"Pleased to meet you." She shook his hand. "Please call me Sarah." She glanced toward the reception area.

"Would you like to wait --"

"He can come in," Gregory said. "I have no objection."

She looked at Gregory for a moment. Her eyes said something about medical confidentiality. Gregory's expression said he understood and had made a considered decision.

She gave a small shrug and led them both inside.

Gregory sat down and became suddenly aware that he was still wearing the sunglasses. He looked momentarily embarrassed -- the particular embarrassment of a man who has been unselfconscious about something and is now very conscious of it. He tucked them into his shirt pocket.

Dr. Okonkwo sat behind her desk. Her posture shifted slightly. More professional. She booted up her computer and spoke as it started.

"As we discussed on the phone, your body is beginning to reject solid food. You'll need a reliable way to ingest bovine plasma to provide the iron and nutrients your system now requires."

She spoke without particular drama, which Gregory appreciated.

"You should begin a daily regimen. Chelated vitamins -- easier on the system than standard pills. Mucinex for the digestive tract. Probiotics and digestive enzymes. The chelated formulations will absorb more efficiently, given what's happening to your system. I would avoid Chelated silver -- it may give you heartburn."

She looked at her screen.

"You'll need at least two litres of liquid daily. To be safe, double that as a working margin. Fourteen litres a week minimum. Twenty-eight to be comfortable."

Gregory was doing the arithmetic. Ted spoke before he finished.

"I've already arranged a local source," Ted said. "Cow blood. Kent abattoir. Ten-gallon containers. I've also sourced an electronic stirrer to prevent coagulation."

Gregory looked at him. He should not have been surprised. He was slightly.

"Good man," he said, under his breath.

Ted gave him a rare smile.

Dr. Okonkwo looked at Ted with the expression of someone recalibrating an assessment.

"Good man," she said.

Ted beamed with pride. Gregory could not remember seeing Ted beam before. It suited him.

"You'll need it warmed to thirty-seven degrees Celsius," she continued. "To avoid thermal shock to the system. A baby bottle warmer will do it, or a small hot plate. Once it's at temperature, mix in the vitamins and sip it steadily. Allow your body to adjust. Any negative reactions -- ring me directly."

She slid a card across the desk, her mobile number written on the back.

"I imagine it will taste terrible," she said.

"Actually, I found it rather pleasant," Gregory said.

Both of them looked surprised.

"It had a metallic taste and was a bit on the salty side, but I could see myself having some at high tea with some scones."

They both laughed. Properly. The kind of laughter that arrives unexpectedly and is better for it.

Ted's eyes crinkled. "We could invite the Duchess of York. For cucumber sandwiches."

"I'm sure Fergie would enjoy a trip to Kent," Dr. Okonkwo said.

The room filled with laughter for a moment -- three very different people finding the same absurdity at the same time. Gregory thought that it was the first time he had laughed, properly laughed, since Thursday evening.

He filed that away, too.

They were on the M20 by noon. Ted drove. Gregory watched the city give way to the home counties and then to Kent, the sky opening up as they went south.

"She's proper," Ted said, somewhere past Maidstone.

"She is," Gregory agreed.

That was the extent of it. Gregory did not need to ask what Ted thought of the situation. Ted had come in, listened to all of it, said the right thing at the right moment, and was now driving home, as though the morning had been entirely ordinary. Which, Gregory supposed, was exactly what he needed.

He thought about the Ephesians verse. Redemption through blood. He had preached on it more than once. He had always understood it as a metaphor -- the language of sacrifice and transformation rendered in the most vivid terms available to a first-century writer.

He was not sure what it was now.

He thought about that for the rest of the drive.

***

The abattoir outside Lydd was a low, functional building set back from the road behind a wire fence, the kind of place that did its work without announcement. Ted had rung ahead. The man who ran it -- broad, practical, few words -- met them at the gate with the first container already loaded on a trolley.

Ten gallons. Tall metal can, two handles, compression lid. The blood inside had been collected that morning. Ted had brought the stirrer motor, already charged, and fitted it to the lid with the efficiency of a man who had thought this through in advance.

The manager watched this with the mild interest of someone who had seen many things and had stopped requiring explanations for most of them.

"Keep it cold -- three to five degrees. Don't let it freeze." He shrugged. "You're not the only ones. Got three others on the same arrangement."

Ted looked up, nodded. Paperwork exchanged. A price agreed that was considerably lower than it should have been, which Gregory suspected was less to do with the medical rationale Ted had offered and more to do with Ted himself, who had the particular quality of inspiring fair dealing in people.

They loaded the can into the boot of the Volvo, which took some doing, and drove back to the church.

Morris Phillips was in the churchyard when they arrived, sitting on the wall by the east gate with a thermos of tea, apparently waiting for nothing in particular. This was not unusual. Morris had a habit of appearing in the churchyard on Sunday afternoons, in the way that people who have been coming to a place for decades develop habits around it.

He watched Ted and Gregory wrestling the can out of the boot with the calm interest of a man who recognised equipment.

"Need help?" Morris said.

"That would be helpful, thanks," Gregory said.

Morris got up from the wall and came over. He and Ted lifted the full can. He looked at Gregory.

"I've got four of those in my barn," Morris said. "Going back to the farming days. No use for them now. Do you want them?"

"That would be very kind, Morris. Thank you."

Morris waved this off. "I'll bring them on Tuesday. Save you buying."

He sat back down on the wall with his thermos. The conversation was over.

Gregory had learned, in eleven years of ministry, that some people expressed generosity the way Morris did -- completely, practically, without requiring acknowledgement beyond the plain acceptance of what was offered.

He accepted it plainly.

***

The vestry refrigerator was a small white appliance of uncertain vintage that had always been slightly too warm for vegetables and slightly too cold for cheese. It had been there when Gregory arrived, and he had never thought much about it.

Ted thought considerably about it.

He removed the vegetable drawer. He removed the egg tray. He took out two of the three shelves and stood them against the vestry wall. He measured the interior dimensions with a tape measure and then measured the milk can and stood for a moment doing arithmetic.

He put the can inside the fridge. It fit with four inches to spare. He attached the stirrer motor to the lid -- it ran off a small rechargeable battery pack, one charge lasting roughly a week.

The fridge door closed. The stirrer hummed. The temperature gauge read four degrees Celsius.

Ted looked at it for a moment with the expression of a man reviewing completed work.

"You'll want a baby bottle warmer," he said. "For when you need it warm. I'll bring one on Tuesday."

"Ted," Gregory said.

"Father."

"Thank you. For all of this."

Ted picked up his tape measure and put it in his pocket.

He went home.

Gregory told Margaret about the fridge that evening, in the careful way Dr. Okonkwo had suggested -- medical requirement, bovine source, blood-derived supplements, weekly delivery. Margaret listened to all of it with the particular quality of attention she gave to things she was filing carefully.

"And the week-old?" she said, when he had finished.

"I suppose it goes off," Gregory said.

Margaret looked at the fridge, then at the roses through the vestry window -- the ones along the church wall that had been struggling since last autumn.

"I'll collect it on Thursdays," she said, "wash it clean so it's dry and ready before Ted brings the new, and the garden could use it."

Gregory said that would be fine.

It was more than fine. Within a month, the roses were extraordinary -- deep red, improbably lush for the season. The tomatoes she had planted against the south-facing vestry wall began to draw comment. By the village show, she had three varieties entered and won two of them, which she accepted with the mild satisfaction of someone who had known this would happen.

***

She never mentioned the blood.

Gregory never asked.

Some arrangements worked best when left unexamined.

***

That evening, Gregory sat in the vestry with the hum of the fridge behind him and a mug of the blood mixture in his hand, the temperature exactly right, and thought about the day.

Ted had sourced the supply before being asked. Morris had donated the cans without needing to know why. Margaret had found a use for what would have been wasted. Dr. Okonkwo had given him her mobile number and laughed at a joke about Fergie.

Nobody had made a fuss.

He thought about Ephesians. Redemption through blood. The riches of his grace.

He was not sure, yet, what his life looked like now. He knew it looked different. He knew it involved a milk can in a repurposed fridge and a stirrer motor on a weekly charge, and a garden that was thriving on things he did not dwell on too long.

He knew it involved Ted saying the same time on Thursday and meaning it.

He thought that might be enough, for now, to be going on with.

He sipped his blood elixir.

Outside, the marsh was going dark. The watercourses caught the last light. Somewhere on the causeway, a car passed, headlights sweeping briefly across the church wall, and was gone.

St Thomas à Becket had been standing in this field since 1200. It had stood through things considerably more difficult than this.

Gregory rather thought it would manage.

Chapter VI -- The Homecoming

"Go home to your friends and tell them how much the Lord has done
for you, and how he has had mercy on you."
-- Mark 5:19

Life shifted into a regular, steady pattern for Gregory.

Every Thursday after services, they would load the clean, dry container into the Volvo, drive to the abattoir, and a new full can would be waiting.

"No charge," said the manager one Thursday morning, as though this had always been the arrangement. "Call it our donation to the church."

Gregory tried to argue. Ted clasped him on the shoulder and thanked the manager.

They drove back to the church, and for some strange reason, lifting the full container was easier for Gregory than before.

"I suppose the additional iron is improving my strength," he said, smiling at Ted.

"I should try your beverage," Ted said.

Gregory said nothing to that. Ted had a way of making observations that were not quite jokes and not quite serious, and required no response at all.

Ted also observed that Gregory was wearing the sunglasses more often, even on cloudy days. He said nothing. He noted it.

Other things were curious about the vicar, though they accumulated so gradually that no one who saw him every day quite registered them as change.

He tended to nap more during the day. He had become something of a night owl. Services were not affected, and no one had any difficulty with access, so it seemed a minor oddity -- the sort of thing one files away under the heading of vicars and their peculiarities.

One morning, Ted stepped out into the yard and glanced up. Gregory was on the roof, near the edge, adjusting a loose slate.

"Morning," Gregory called down, as if it were the most ordinary thing in the world.

Ted nodded. Then he looked along the side of the church. He looked at the other side. He looked at the churchyard wall, the gate, and the vestry door.

There was no ladder.

"How'd you get up there?"

"Climbed up. Saw the hanging slate."

Ted shaded his eyes for a moment, as though he might have missed something. Then he lowered his hand.

"Careful up there," he said.

"Of course," Gregory replied.

Ted gave a small nod and went inside. He did glance back once. He noted that too.

Another morning, they were walking along the water for their constitutional. Ted was talking about the local paper coming to photograph Margaret's garden. He looked up mid-sentence.

Gregory was three hundred paces ahead of him. A moment before, they had been side by side.

"You're daydreaming again, old codger. Pay more attention," Ted thought.

Later, Ted was mounting a shelf in the vestry.

"Vicar, can you lend a hand?"

He looked to his left. Gregory was standing beside him.

"Of course," Gregory said, taking hold of the other end.

The days settled back into their usual rhythm. Ted filed everything away in the part of his mind reserved for things that did not yet require action.

***

"I've a follow-up in London on Thursday," Gregory said one evening. "Some results to go over."

Ted nodded. "I won't be about -- I'm going into Ealing to see my brother. You'll have to take the train, I'm afraid."

"That will be perfectly fine."

"Margaret said she'll drop you and pick you up at the station."

"Very kind of her."

"They're dropping the delivery in the morning. Margaret will sign for it."

"Quite right."

Of course, Ted had handled it. He always did.

The morning service was abuzz with news. The Archdeacon from St Mary's would be visiting to observe Margaret's award-winning garden.

He was a large, stout Irishman with naturally rosy cheeks that gave him the look of someone who had just stepped out of a pub rather than a church. He greeted them warmly, admired the roses, asked after the tomatoes, and spoke at length with Margaret about the soil and the season and the particular vigour of the blooms.

It was only after a time that his attention settled on Gregory.

There was a pause. Small, but noticeable.

"Are you all right?" he asked. "You look quite pale."

And he was pale -- but the change had happened so slowly that no one who saw him every day had noticed. Not even Ted and Margaret, who observed everything. The skin had shifted by degrees, too gradual for daily familiarity to register.

Gregory inclined his head. "Yes. I was bitten a few months back. I'm going to London for treatments."

"Is it helping?"

"The doctor has put me on a strict diet," Gregory said. "She says I'm stable."

The Archdeacon regarded him for a moment longer, then gave a small nod.

"Good," he said. "That's good. In the English countryside, wild things run fast." Gregory smiled. "They do," he agreed.

Thursday morning's sermon was on the path one takes in life.

Trust in the Lord with all your heart and lean not on your own understanding; in all your ways submit to him, and he will make your paths straight.

It seemed Gregory was practising what he preached.

The train journey to London was rather enjoyable. Margaret had packed him a thermos, and he sipped from it as the train carried him along, surrounded by dozens of others enjoying their own version of blood.

His time in the city was brief. For whatever reason, London seemed busier than usual -- everyone moving a bit faster: the traffic, the people, even their speech. He found it disconcerting, as though he were moving at a different pace than the rest of the world. He thought about this on the platform at Charing Cross and concluded, without particular distress, that he probably was.

He saw Dr. Okonkwo. The results were, she said, consistent with the previous panel -- the changes were stabilising, which was the best they had hoped for. He took the train home.

She was already seated across from him when he settled into his carriage -- or he had not noticed her until she was, which amounted to the same thing. A tall woman in a Dior business suit, composed and still in the way of someone accustomed to being very still for very long periods. She smelled of lemons.

She was looking at him.

Not the way passengers look at one another on trains -- the polite, deflecting glance. She was looking at him with the focused attention of someone reading something.

He looked back.

She saw the telltale marks on his neck. Human eyes would have seen nothing; the skin had healed without a trace. But she was not looking with human eyes. She was reading the particular signature of what he was -- human, yes, but also something else. And the timing was wrong. He had been bitten and had not transformed. Had remained, somehow, in between.
The fact that he had not transformed both delighted and frightened her.

She moved to sit beside him.

"Father, may I ask you something?"

Gregory put on his best pastoral face. He also noted, quietly, that there was more here than met the eye. Something in her stillness. Something in the quality of her attention.

"Of course," he said. "What can I help you with?"

"Why are you on a train to the Marshlands?" she said. "All that is out there are dreary castles and opinionated sheep."

Gregory laughed warmly. "I have a small parish there. In Kent. St Thomas à Becket, Fairfield."

Something shifted in her expression. Very slight.

"Oh," she said. "That's Sir Edmund's territory."

She heard herself say it. A fractional pause -- the pause of someone who has said more than they intended.

She changed course smoothly. "I expect the spring roses will be coming in soon. It's said to be spectacular."

Gregory let it go. He filed it away --

"Yes," he said pleasantly. "Our caretaker Margaret has been rather pleased with them."

"And where are you headed?" Gregory asked.

"Leeds Castle," she said. "I have business there. Afterwards -- might I visit your parish?"

"You are more than welcome," Gregory said. "It would be an honour."

"What line of work are you in, if I may enquire?"

"Pharmaceuticals," she said. Gregory nodded. Of course.

They sat in companionable silence as the train moved south through Kent, the city giving way to the home counties and then to the flatlands, the sky opening up, the landscape becoming older and quieter and more itself.

She looked out the window. He looked out the window. Neither spoke again until the train slowed for Ashford.
"Umbra Shadows," she said, as she stood. She offered her hand.

"Father Gregory Chadwick."

"Pleasure." She nodded and was gone.

Gregory sat alone in the carriage as the train pulled into the station. He thought about her comment and what that meant. He thought about a woman in a Dior suit who worked in pharmaceuticals.

The marsh was waiting. The church was waiting. Margaret would be at the station with the car. He got off the train.

Chapter VII -- The Sojourner

"Do not forget to show hospitality to strangers, for by so doing some people have shown hospitality to angels without knowing it." --
Hebrews 13:2

Umbra Shadows arrived mid-afternoon at the church. It was a forty minute taxi ride from Leeds, and she was surprised she had never heard of this delightful hamlet or the small church by the water.

Gregory gave her a tour of the church, the grounds, the flowers, and the garden.

The church was a delight. As they stepped inside, she took it in, her gaze moving along the walls, from base to ceiling -- like an architect appreciating a completed work. Gregory noted this but made no comment.

Most people looked at the white pews, the tall staging. She assessed the dimensions of the building rather than the beauty of what it contained.

"Built around 1200?" she asked, already knowing she was accurate.

"Spot on," Gregory said. "You know your history."

They sat and settled into a pew, its wood polished and warm.

Margaret came in with a teapot of warm red tea, the smell aromatic and metallic.

"What is that you're drinking? It smells delightful."

"I'm on a limited diet," Gregory said. "It's one of the few things I can sip and enjoy."

"I smell the honey -- just the correct amount. May I have a cup?"

Margaret said, "You may not like it. It's not normal tea."

Umbra grinned. "Of course it isn't. You're using cow blood."

Both of them looked at her.

"And you still want a cup?"

Margaret shrugged, placed an empty teacup in front of her, and poured.

Umbra took a sip, closed her eyes.

"I haven't had a proper cup of tea in a decade." She smiled warmly.

Margaret piped up, "It was Nana's recipe."

Margaret set the teapot down and looked between them, her expression unchanged, as if noting something already decided. Her eyes lingered on Umbra for a moment, then shifted to Gregory. She studied him more closely, not with surprise, but with a kind of quiet assessment.

"Well," she said softly, looking at Umbra.

"You're a vampire."

Her gaze moved to Gregory.

A small pause.

"You're not quite there yet."

They both sat stunned. Umbra had spent twenty lifetimes perfecting her identity, yet at a glance, this woman knew everything about her. She was shocked -- but absolutely delighted.

"The moment you walked in, I knew. You were the exact memory of my nana, who was a vampire. At the time, I did not know that. It took me fifty years to understand it. But as soon as you wanted the tea, I knew. It was my nana's favourite drink, and sipping it, you had the same expression."

At that moment, there were voices at the door -- a woman crying and a man trying to comfort her. Gregory rose quickly.

"Please excuse me."

He hurried off.

***

"My nana used to make tea like this," Margaret said, almost to herself.

Umbra glanced up, but said nothing.

"I was very small. Five, perhaps. She was always... around, and then she wasn't."

"Years passed. I didn't see her at all."

A pause.

"Then she came to my graduation."

Margaret gave a small, private smile.

"She didn't look a day older."

"How did you become who you are?" Margaret's face was open with curiosity.

Umbra, who was usually very private, opened up to this warm human.

"I was born in 1805, the daughter of a man who worked for the Stockton and Darlington, helping build the first steam engines to carry trains across England. Growing up, I was always around his work -- his tools, diagrams, parts. They were the things I played with, not dolls. Bottles that once held battery oil --"

"I was something of a tomboy, fascinated that a bit of water and heat could create something powerful enough to move twenty tons of steel."

She looked at her hands.

"I still have the callouses."

She showed Margaret.

"I was bitten in 1830, walking down a street in Highgate. Attacked by a vampire, I bit him in return, trying to defend myself. He was so impressed by my cheekiness that he made me his protégé."

A pause.

"He was an excellent teacher."

"I stayed with this man for many years. He was a teacher when he was still..." She paused, remembering. "But he was very angry at humanity and killed without need. He was more interested in quiet than human life." She frowned at the memory.

Margaret was quiet for a moment. "And you stayed?"

Umbra gave a small nod. "I learned what he had to teach."

A slight pause.

"And I learned what to leave behind."

She folded her hands.

"I now work for a person who is deeply interested in helping humanity. For the past hundred years, he has helped pioneer public health, ensuring polio vaccinations reached every child. He had been the backbone of public health long before there was even an institution for it."

Margaret tilted her head slightly. "That's... quite a change."

"Yes." Umbra's voice remained even. "It was a choice."

A brief silence.

"From him, I learned compassion -- for all God's creatures, great and small."

"He has created a human blood replacement, based on the same ingredients in your delightful tea -- though I must admit, I would love the addition of honey to its formulation. It is what I, and several hundred of us, live on. I have not drawn human blood in over a quarter of a century."

"Tell me about the vicar." Umbra's face took on a serious look.

"Before, you said, 'You're not quite there yet.'"

Margaret was taken aback that she had been quoted verbatim. This was a woman who remembered details.

"I have fragments of the whole story. What seems to have transpired was that, after a Thursday sermon, a man came into the church. They chatted a bit. He attacked the father. He had just lit a kettle of water, and the whistle of it boiling distracted the vampire long enough for him to repel him with his crucifix."

Umbra's expression flashed a change; she corrected it quickly. Crosses and symbols meant nothing to her kind -- it would be the equivalent of holding up a feather.

Margaret continued, "He had the forethought to use antiseptic on the wound and saw a doctor the next day. I believe that combination prevented the infection from spreading. He was sent immediately to a blood specialist in London, who monitored his blood chemistry and kept adjusting the formulation to match his nutritional needs."

Umbra could not hide the look of total joy on her face. "He was stabilised immediately. The infection was put in check."

She suddenly stood. "I'm sorry, I need to make a call. I will return in ten minutes."

She glanced at Gregory, still talking with the now much calmer couple.

***

She returned as promised. Gregory was just saying goodbye to the couple and was walking back to them.

"Bit of an issue with their dog -- hit by a lorry. Luckily, the poor thing was small and was more pushed than impacted. Nothing was broken. He was just stunned."

Margaret seemed relieved. "A dog isn't an animal; it is a family member."

***

"We were having a chat about your 'incident,'" Umbra said. "Would you give me your impression of what transpired?"

Gregory shifted uncomfortably for a moment but continued.

"It was a Thursday evening," Gregory said. "After the service. A man came in through the door. We talked for a while -- he declined tea. His name was Edmund."

Umbra was very still.

"Did he give you his surname?"

"No," said Gregory. "But I am assuming it was the same Edmund you mentioned on the train."

Umbra frowned. "You heard that."

Gregory gave a small smile. "In my line of work, you learn quickly that what people say in passing is often the most important thing they say. It is a skill one develops out of necessity. They do not teach it in theological college -- but they should."

"When he attacked me, I defended myself with my crucifix." He pointed to the crucifix hanging from his neck -- heavy, dark with age, one edge worn sharper by time. Umbra immediately focused her vision on it and saw the blood in the grain, the angle it had entered

Edmund's chest at a 45-degree pitch, that one worn edge sharp enough to pierce the breastbone and reach the heart. And the strength that drove it home -- not chosen, not trained. Terror and adrenaline, and a body doing what bodies do in the moment, everything is on the line.

"And this transpired some nine weeks ago?" she asked.

"Yes," Gregory replied.

"I heard it -- a single, sharp report. At the time, I did not register that it was the end of Sir Edmund of Warwick. Rest in peace, dear sir -- you were an honourable man." Umbra spoke in an almost hushed tone.

Gregory suddenly remembered something, went to a cabinet, and opened a drawer. He pulled out a small object that looked metallic and handed it to Umbra.

"This was what remained after he turned to dust."

She unravelled what looked like a coiled necklace. The metal links were worn over time. "This was the remains of his coif," Umbra said sadly. "He wore it every day to remind him what he was."

Margaret, who had been very silent, quietly asked, "So he was a knight?"

Umbra looked at Margaret and said, "No. He was the knight."

***

Chapter VIII -- The Rephuah

"Consider the lilies" -- Matthew 6:28

About forty-five minutes later, a Rolls-Royce Phantom appeared at the end of the causeway.

Gregory and Umbra were standing outside the church when they saw it approaching -- black, gleaming, moving slowly along the narrow road.

"Now this is not what you see every day," Gregory said, more to himself than to her. "The most expensive vehicle ever in front of this church has been Ted's Volvo."

Umbra chuckled softly.

The car pulled up. The door opened.

The man who emerged was not what Gregory expected. Eighty, perhaps, with white hair quite bright in the afternoon light. But the age stopped there. He moved with the assurance of someone who played tennis every morning -- posture perfect, walk graceful, the kind of physical vitality that made the number seem wrong. Healthy complexion. Mild age spots on his face. Otherwise, he could have been fifty.

He smiled warmly as he approached.

"I would like to introduce you to my friend and benefactor, Kushim Arit," Umbra said. "He is two thousand years old."

The man's smile widened. "Please, call me Carey. There are two of us left -- myself and Mel Brooks."

He chuckled -- the laugh had texture to it, like sandpaper.

Gregory laughed. Genuinely. The joke landed, disarming and warm.

Carey extended his hand. Gregory shook it -- firm, confident, the grip of someone who had shaken hands for two thousand years and knew exactly how much pressure to apply.

Gregory noted the irony. Two vampires are standing in front of a church in the sunlight. He filed this away.

"Would you care to see the church?" Gregory asked.

"I would be delighted," Carey said. There was something in the way he said it -- not polite interest, but genuine enthusiasm. As though he had been waiting for this.

They walked toward the door. Carey paused at the threshold. His hand reached out, fingers brushing the timber frame -- not examining it, but touching it the way you might touch something familiar. Something you remembered.

"This old gal," he said softly. "She has quite a history."

Said with affection. Fondness, even.

They ducked through -- everyone bowed at St Thomas à Becket, even two-thousand-year-old vampires -- and stepped inside.

"They lowered the entrance ways to hold in the heat during winter," Carey said, almost to himself. Not showing off. Just remembering.

Gregory felt something shift in his chest. The way Carey said it -- casual, certain. That kind of detail. This wasn't from a book.

Carey moved slowly into the church, his eyes travelling along the walls, from base to ceiling. Taking it in the way Umbra had -- but deeper, longer, as though seeing layers Gregory could not see. Time layered on time.

He walked a few steps further in, his gaze moving across the white box pews, the triple-decker pulpit, and the particular light coming through the small windows.

"Romney Marsh," Carey said. "Between Sissinghurst and Rye, East Sussex."

He touched the wall lightly.

"Built circa 1200 as a temporary timber structure. Temporary became permanent."

Gregory's hand found a pew. He kept listening. Completely.

Carey moved along the wall, fingers brushing the surface. "Eighteenth century -- they encased it in brick. Gave it a proper roof. Heavy red tiles."

He walked further, getting more animated as he went. "1912... they rebuilt it entirely within the timber frame. Left the interior untouched."

His eyes lifted toward the ceiling. "Georgian interior. Theatrical. Unexpected. Box pews painted bright white. Triple-decker pulpit."

A pause. He turned slightly, looking back toward the door.

"They built the causeway in 1913. Before that, winter and spring, it was unreachable. Isolated."

Another pause.

"Still is, in a way."

Gregory found himself smiling slightly. Every detail Carey gave was accurate. But it was more than that. This wasn't history. This was memory.

Carey turned toward Gregory, his expression warm. "Patron saint -- Thomas Becket. Murdered in his own cathedral... by instruments of the institution he served, Henry the second was he was a right bastard"

He let that sit for a moment.

"That is not a coincidence."

A faint, knowing look.

"Places like this... they tend to choose their own stories."

Gregory said nothing. His pastoral training held -- he listened, completely, without interrupting. But underneath, both things were happening at once: wonder at hearing living history, and fear at what it meant that this was real. That vampires were not theoretical. That the ground had shifted beneath his feet.

He filed it all away. To be returned to later.

Umbra watched both of them quietly. Professional. Pleased to see her employer so animated. She said nothing.

***

"Shall we sit?" Gregory said, finally.

They settled into one of the white box pews, the wood smooth and warm beneath them. Carey looked entirely at ease, as though he had sat in churches like this for centuries.

Which, Gregory thought, he probably had.

Carey smiled. "Now then," he said, his voice taking on a different quality -- storytelling mode.

"Let me tell you how I got here. I was born in 26 AD. I was seven years old when they crucified Christ. In my adult life, I was a healer. They dug me out of Pompeii in 1863."

A pause.

"I have been existing on fetal bovine serum since the 1960s. I own many of the labs in the region and have become quite rich -- just trying to keep myself fed, ethically."

He looked at his hands.

"I have spent over a thousand years keeping myself alive. When I heard about you from Umbra, I wanted to meet you. You have a unique condition of being a mid-tier vampire. You are still human, yet you have the vampire DNA living in you, coexisting."

"Your blood may reveal secrets that have been hidden for all of those years."

Carey met Gregory's eyes.

"I started thinking you may be the key to letting me die -- peacefully."

The marsh light came through the small windows. Outside, somewhere, a sheep made a considered remark about something.

Gregory sat with this. The way he sat with everything -- patiently, without rushing to fill the silence.

"When Umbra told me about you," Carey continued, "I began investigating. I saw the mRNA research that Dr. Okonkwo has been doing. I saw the fact that you are in this mid-tier -- you remain human. You sleep, you eat, you age. It has given me the first ray of hope in over a hundred years."

He paused.

"I have also been told about who bit you. Edmund was a good lad. He had a troubled past -- he could never settle with it."

Carey's voice softened slightly.

"I was glad for him when I heard he had been given the yetziat neshamah."

Carey's voice softened further. "It's what I've been seeking myself. A peaceful end, after all these years, the yetziat neshamah."

"The departure of the soul," Gregory said quietly. He knew Hebrew – it was required reading in theological college, and he had also read books of other faiths over the years. Understanding them helped him understand his own.

Carey nodded. "A peaceful death. What Edmund had been seeking for the last eight centuries." Gregory thought about the thunderclap. The dust was settling into the crevices of the flagstone floor. Edmund's last words: Thank you. The shock, then the delight.

"Gregory," Carey said. "May I have your permission to have Dr. Okonkwo's files and research sent over to one of my labs in London? And also your permission to have blood drawn, if needed? I will, of course, pay for all transport and accommodations."

Gregory did not pause. "I will phone her in the morning."

Carey's smile widened into something brighter. "You have no idea," he said softly. "After all this time... you may be the answer I've been searching for."

A small pause. "One last thing -- you should, at some point, check the cellar."

Gregory blinked. "We don't have a cellar."

Carey smiled. The kind of smile that contained two thousand years of knowing things other people did not. "Yes," he said gently. "You do."

***

Chapter IX -- The Revelation

*"And when I passed by thee, and saw thee polluted in thine own blood,
I said unto thee when thou wast in thy blood, Live; yea, I said unto thee
when thou wast in thy blood, Live." -- Ezekiel 16:6*

Gregory's call came mid-morning.

"Good morning, Sarah. I wanted to let you know you may be contacted regarding my medical records. Bloodwork, tests, anything you have on file. Please give them access to whatever they require."

There was nothing unusual in his tone.

"Of course," she said. "Who should I expect?"

"A research group. I'll explain more when I see you."

A small pause.

"I will phone you later," Gregory added, and ended the call.

***

Dr. Okonkwo sat for a moment, the receiver still in her hand. Nothing in what he said was improper. Patients granted access all the time. Still... something about the call felt incomplete, as though a piece had been left out.

She set it aside and returned to her work.

Thirty-five minutes later, there was a knock at the door.

A courier stood outside, envelope in hand.

"Dr. Okonkwo?"

"Yes."

"I have a delivery for you, miss."

She signed, took the envelope, and turned it over once in her hands. No markings beyond her name. Heavy paper.

The courier did not leave.

"I have been asked to wait, if that's no trouble, miss."

She looked at him, then back at the envelope.

"Of course," she said. "Please, sit."

She opened it carefully.

The letter inside was brief. Formal. Direct.

The name at the top was one she recognised immediately.

The Plasma Institute.

She read it once.

Then again, more slowly.

A small shift in posture.

She set the paper down, then picked it up again, as if confirming it had not changed between readings.

"I've read their articles in the medical journals..." she said quietly to herself.

This wasn't written by a nurse, or even a doctor. It was written by a haematopathologist -- highly specialised in the field, with molecular detail on exactly what was being sought.

Access to all relevant data. Immediate transfer requested. Full authorisation acknowledged.

She reached for Gregory's file.

Minutes passed in silence.

She reviewed prior bloodwork, scanning values she had already seen, now reading them with a different weight. Small irregularities. Patterns that had seemed incidental -- noted, but not pursued.

Her expression did not change, but her attention sharpened.

She closed the file.

It took two thumb drives.

One for lab results.

The other for imaging, photographs, and clinical data.

She worked methodically, verifying each transfer and labelling each device.

No shortcuts. No assumptions.

When she returned to the door, the courier was exactly where she had left him.

He accepted the drives without comment.

"I can arrange reimbursement for any expenses," he said.

She gave a small laugh.

"It's less than ten quid. I think I can handle it."

A faint nod.

"Thank you, miss."

He turned and left.

The door closed.

Dr. Okonkwo stood for a moment, her hand still resting on the handle.

Then she walked back to her desk and looked at Gregory's file again.

Not as a patient.

But as something else.

The phone rang.

"Dr. Okonkwo."

"Sarah, it's Gregory."

A brief pause -- recognition.

"Gregory. I was expecting you might call."

"Yes." A small breath. "Did everything arrive without issue?"

"It did. Your friends are... thorough."

"I believe they are," Gregory said. "And I believe their intentions are noble."

A quiet moment settled between them.

"They seem very interested in you," she added.

"I believe they are," he said again, more softly.

A slight shift -- hard to place, but present.

"Sarah," he continued, "I would like to update you on the circumstances."

Her attention sharpened.

"Of course."

"I would prefer we speak in person," he said. "Somewhere public. Quiet, if possible. Halfway between us."

A beat.

"There's a small pub in Snargate," he said. "The Red Lion. Ted takes his wife there."

"That would be suitable."

Another pause.

"Gregory," she said carefully, "is there something I should know?"

A breath. Measured.

"No," he said. "Nothing that requires immediate attention... but the world has become much larger."

And then, after a moment:

"But I would rather not discuss it over the telephone."

That settled it.

"I understand," she said.

"I'll see you shortly."

The line went quiet.

***

Gregory sat in the back of a cab, staring out the window at the Kent countryside sliding past. When had he stopped driving? He had not really thought about it before. Ted had always been there to ferry him -- same time Thursday, trips to London, the abattoir runs. He had been living in a bubble.

His tongue found the tooth again. The growing tooth. He pressed against it, felt the sharp edge. It had become more annoying in the past week. A persistent reminder every time he swallowed, every time he spoke. He must consult a dentist and have this addressed.

The cab driver swerved around a lorry. Gregory barely registered it.

He watched the world blur past -- hedgerows, sheep, the occasional cottage. All of it is familiar. All of it felt somehow distant now, as though he were watching it through glass.

He thought about a shepherd's pie at the pub. He had not had a good shepherd's pie in...

Oh.

He couldn't eat it.

He lived on blood now.

Maybe it was temporary. Just a condition that would be cured. Dr. Okonkwo was brilliant. The research Carey mentioned. The labs. Surely they would find something. Reverse it. Fix it.

The tooth pressed against his tongue.

Temporary.

He thought about who he served. Eleven years at St Thomas à Becket. Vows taken young with genuine conviction. He had been faithful. Served his congregation. Done the work.

Why him?

He filed the question away. Not his place to ask. Just move forward. Keep calm and carry on. One Thursday at a time.

This was his path now. He did not understand it. But he could accept it.

Let go and let God.

The cab pulled up outside The Red Lion.

***

She arrived exactly fifty minutes after the phone conversation. Gregory arrived five minutes later. He was in a hired cab, wearing street clothing -- a cardigan and trousers. She had never noticed how handsome he was. She had always seen him as a priest -- male, never as a man.

Seeing her, he smiled. Pointing to the cab.

"This isn't church business, and no business of the Church."

They went inside and sat toward the back. The place had just finished serving lunch, and the staff were eating their own meals, leaving them to themselves.

A waitress appeared. She ordered a pint of Guinness. He ordered water.

Sarah looked into his eyes. They appeared a bit red, almost as if he had been crying.

"What is going on? Your phone call caused me some consternation."

It took a moment for Gregory to compose his words. He had been thinking of them on the way to the pub, in the back of the cab.

"My condition... have you ever named it?"

She looked up. "You have a blood-borne pathogen caused by a bite that has altered your body's functions."

"And what would you call that in layman's terms?" he asked.

"You have an infection that has made physiological changes to your body," Sarah replied, curiosity lining her face.

"I am a vampire," Gregory said, in all seriousness.

Sarah laughed -- a good, hearty laugh. "I should not have ordered the garlic bread," she jested.

Gregory smiled. "Think about it. The diet. The shutdown of functions. The enhancement of strength and senses... the sensitivity to light."

Sarah shook her head. "Vampires are what you watch on the telly when you are looking for sexual thrills and violence. This is not some fantasy; this is all very serious. I researched the Plasma Institute. The Arit Foundation, who owns it, has been in medical research as long as there has been one. In 1910, they were the first to stop using mercury and to use Salvarsan to aid in the treatment of syphilis and trypanosomiasis."

"And later?" Gregory asked.

"And later," Sarah continued, "they helped find cures for malaria, hepatitis. They have been very much involved in researching Zika, HIV, Ebola..."

"And what do they all have in common?" Gregory asked.

She paused, her face changing as she realised.

"They are all blood-based."

"Exactly," Gregory said.

"I met the older Arit yesterday. He visited the church."

"Is he the grandson? The great-grandson of the founder?"

"No. I met Kushim Arit -- the founder."

Sarah laughed. "That man would be dust. He was in his eighties in 1910. You're lying."

And Sarah's face did something strange. She realised Gregory doesn't lie or embellish. He speaks plainly and honestly.

Her expression changed, and she said, "You're ly..."

She could not finish the statement, because she knew he was telling the truth -- nay, stating it as a fact.

She went silent. Gregory understood this moment. He had seen it many times -- in church, in confession -- when a truth suddenly appears and sits down.

She downed her pint of Guinness, in hopes it would wash away some of the reality assaulting her. She thought about ordering another when Gregory said, as if he was reading her mind, "Remember, you are driving."

She smiled and said, "You are displaying vampire powers... count."

Gregory laughed, softly at first. Then the laugh deepened as the reality of his own words settled in his brain. He laughed so hard that his chest shook, and a tear fell from his eye -- a single, red, blood tear.

Sarah looked at it in shock, then quickly dabbed her napkin in his water and wiped it away.

She recovered, but her thoughts were racing. "You have been honest. You have always been honest. I should have never doubted that," she said. "And I believe you."

Gregory nodded. He was still struggling with it -- the simple way Margaret had said it, so matter-of-fact, no nonsense, the truth unfiltered.

"Are we? Am I in any peril?" Sarah asked suddenly.

"I do not think so. They have been benevolent for over a century. Carey -- Mr. Arit -- and his associate were polite, honest, and forward. But they are vampires, and there are new rules at play, and we need to be aware that the game has changed..."

***

Chapter X -- 'X' Marks the Spot

"He is like a man which built an house, and digged deep, and laid the foundation on a rock." -- Luke 6:48

Gregory asked Ted to stay after the Thursday blood run. They sat in the vestry, the communion vessels put away, the church quiet.

Gregory had been thinking about this conversation for weeks. How to explain. Where to begin. But Ted had earned the truth, and Gregory wouldn't insult him with half-measures.

"The attack," Gregory said. "It wasn't random."

Ted waited.

"Sir Edmund of Warwick. He was... he was a vampire. Had been for eight centuries. He came to me seeking peace. I gave him what he asked for though I did not know it at the time." Gregory paused. "The blood deliveries. The medical condition. I'm not quite human anymore. Not quite... the other thing. Dr Okonkwo calls it Perdition's Doorway. The middle state."

Ted nodded slowly.

"There are others," Gregory continued. "Vampires. Real. Not the things from films. Just... people who've lived a very long time. One visited recently. His name is Carey. Two thousand years old. He's seeking the same peace Edmund found. Before he left, he said something odd. Told me we should check the cellar."

Gregory stopped. Waited. Gave Ted space to process, to question, to react.

Ted was quiet for a long moment, the way he got when filing something away in the part of his mind that didn't yet require action.

Then: "Makes sense."

Gregory blinked. "That's... that's it?"

"Well." Ted considered. "You were attacked. You survived. Been drinking blood since. Still doing your job. Still the same man. Makes sense there'd be more to it." He paused. "And we don't have a cellar. Or didn't think we did. So if this Carey fellow says we do, it might be worth a look."

"You're not... concerned?"

"About what?"

"About any of this."

Ted shrugged. "You're still Gregory. Still Father Chadwick. Still show up every Sunday. That's what matters." He stood. "Right. I'll have a proper look round then, shall I? Got a few hours Tuesday."

Gregory felt something tight in his chest loosen. "Thank you, Ted."

"Might as well," Ted said. "Nothing else pressing on."

***

Tuesday came. Ted arrived with his toolkit and a tape measure, the sort of methodical preparation he brought to everything. His dog came with him, a border collie with one ear that refused to stand up properly, sniffing at the corners Ted hadn't touched in years.

"Out of it, boy," Ted said, not unkindly, as the dog investigated a gap between two pews.

He started with the obvious places. The vestry cupboards. The space beneath the organ. The corners where the walls met the floor. Tapping. Listening. Measuring the interior against the exterior dimensions, he'd walked dozens of times.

Nothing obvious presented itself.

"Well," he said to the dog, who'd given up investigating and settled by the font. "Proper search wants proper time."

He went home for lunch. Walked the dog. Came back on Wednesday if he had time.

***

The first find came on a Friday.

Ted had decided to do the thing properly, which meant moving the pews one section at a time. Clean them. Check beneath them. Put them back. The missus came along that afternoon and helped him shift one of the older benches.

"What's this then?" she said, reaching into the gap.

A coin. Blackened with patina but solid. Ted turned it over in his palm.

"Look," he said, showing her. "Edward on a shilling."

"Which Edward?"

He squinted at it. "Third, I think. Maybe 1760s."

She smiled. "Someone dropped their collection money."

"Two hundred and sixty years ago." Ted examined it more closely. "Worth a few hundred quid now, I'd reckon." He wrapped it carefully in a handkerchief and made a note in his book. Date found. Location. Description. Theodore Holmes, on the case.

The missus kissed his cheek and went home to put the kettle on. Ted kept working.

***

The discoveries accumulated.

A child's toy soldier, missing one leg. Found wedged behind the baptismal font, probably dropped in the 1800s. Ted wrapped it with the same care he'd given the coin.

Three more coins. George III. Victoria. Edward VII. Centuries of loose change finding the cracks.

A prayer card, the ink faded, but the pressed flower inside was still holding its shape. Someone's bookmark, left behind.

Old hymnals, spine cracked, pages brittle. He set those aside for the Diocese to assess.

And Bibles. Everywhere, Bibles. Mice had dined on some. Water damage had ruined others. But tucked in a cupboard he'd opened a hundred times before and somehow never looked properly inside, Ted found one in remarkable condition. The leather was cracked, the pages yellowed, but intact. He opened it carefully.

1611. King James.

He sat down right there on the floor, the dog settling beside him, and just looked at it. Four hundred years old. The same words Gregory read every Sunday.

The same book, handed down, preserved. Worth more than his car. Worth more than a year's salary. Someone had cared for this. Someone had wrapped it, stored it, kept it safe through wars and weather and the long centuries.

Ted sealed it carefully in a preservation bag he'd brought for just such a find. "This is one the vicar needs to deal with," he said to the dog. Made his note. Went home for tea.

When Margaret heard about it two days later, her eyes went distant for just a moment.

"That would pay for a new organ," she said.

Margaret started bringing him sandwiches.

"You'll work yourself to death," she said, appearing with a proper tea tray on a Wednesday afternoon.

"Just having a look round," Ted said.

"For three months."

"Takes as long as it takes." He accepted the tea gratefully. Two tuts. The dog got a proper dog biscuit.

On a particularly warm Saturday in late spring, she brought him a beer.

"Don't tell the vicar," she said.

"Gregory won't mind."

"I know. I'm telling you not to tell him so you feel properly scandalised about it."

Ted held the beer up high.

"Lord, bless this creature, beer, which by your kindness and power has been produced from kernels of grain, and let it be a healthful drink for mankind. Grant that whoever drinks it with thanksgiving to your holy name may find it a help in body and in soul; through Christ our Lord."

Ted smiled and drank his beer. Margaret tutted at the dust and went back to her roses.

***

By month three, Ted had worked his way around most of the church. The pews had been moved, cleaned, catalogued, and returned. His notebook was filling up with finds and observations. Nothing earthshattering. Just the accumulated layers of a building that had stood for eight hundred years.

Which brought him, finally, to the panelled wall on the right side of the nave, about midway down.

Heavy tapestries hung over it, faded and dusty. They'd been there since before Ted became churchwarden. Everyone assumed there was storm damage underneath, something that would need addressing eventually. Eventually had become thirty years of never quite getting round to it.

"Right then," Ted said to the dog. "Let's have a look."

He took the tapestries down carefully. They were old. Possibly valuable. Certainly heavy. The missus came by and helped him fold them properly.

"Need to get these cleaned," he said, examining them.

"Can't imagine that's cheap."

"Probably not."

He rang a textile restoration specialist on Monday. The quote came back on Wednesday.

Thirty thousand pounds.

Ted looked at the number. Looked at the tapestries. Looked at his dog.

"Right," he said.

He drove to the shop in the village and bought a bottle of dry dog shampoo for six pounds. Came home. Laid the tapestries out carefully in his garage. Followed the instructions on the bottle. Worked the powder through the fabric gently, methodically, section by section. Let it sit. Brushed it out.

They came up beautifully.

The missus found him in the garage that evening, quietly pleased with himself.

"Six quid," he said.

She kissed the top of his head. "Course it was."

***

The panelling underneath was dark wood, old but well-preserved. No storm damage at all. Just... panelling. Plain. Unremarkable.

Ted ran his hand along it, the way he'd done with every surface in the church by now. Learning its texture. Feeling for anything unusual.

The dog sat beside him, watching. Then, without warning, it started sniffing at the base of the panel. Insistent. The way he got when he'd found something interesting on their walks.

"What've you got, boy?"

Ted tapped the panel where the dog was sniffing.

Hollow.

He tapped again. Definitely hollow. He moved his hand along the panel, tapping systematically. The sound changed halfway across. Solid wood. Then hollow again. Then solid.

His pulse quickened slightly, though he'd never admit it. He fetched his torch, examined the edges. There. A seam. Not decorative. Functional.

He worked one panel loose carefully. It came away easier than expected, like it had been opened before.

Behind it: darkness. Stone. The smell of old wet air.

Ted shone his torch inside.

A stone archway. Roman stonework, clearly. Steps descending. And just beyond, what looked like a small chamber. Stone bench. The suggestion of carvings on the walls.

He stood there for a long moment, torch in hand, dog pressing against his leg.

"Well," he said quietly. "There it is then."

He rang Gregory.

"Father," Ted said. "I think I've found the entrance."

"You're certain?"

"Archway. Midsection behind the panelling. I've had a look with the torch. There's a chamber -- looks like a confessional, maybe. Stone bench. And a stairwell going down from there. I'd need proper lights to see much more."

Silence on the other end. Then: "I'll be right there."

***

They descended together with proper torches. The confessional chamber was small, carved from stone. Simple. A bench worn smooth by centuries of use. The walls bore Roman carvings, faint but unmistakable.

Beyond it, stairs continued down into darkness.

Gregory stood in the small chamber, taking it in. The air was cool. Old. Undisturbed.

"This is beyond us, Ted."

Ted nodded. "Thought as much."

"We need professionals. I won't have centuries of work damaged by our carelessness." Gregory looked at the stairs, the carvings, the careful stonework. "This is history."

"I'll ring the local paper," Ted said. "They'll know who to contact."

"Good man."

The paper came the next day. Photographer. Journalist. Questions about when it was found, what they'd seen so far, and whether they'd gone further down.

Ted explained it all methodically. The months of searching. The panelled wall. The confessional chamber. The stairs continue into darkness. No, they hadn't gone further. Waiting for the proper people.

The article ran that Friday. "Roman Discovery Beneath Romney Marsh Church." Accompanying photographs of the stone archway, the carvings, and Ted standing beside the opening with his usual solid expression.

The paper contacted an archaeologist. She arrived the following week with Ground Penetrating Radar equipment.

What the GPR revealed made her stop and recalibrate the equipment twice.

The structure beneath St Thomas à Becket was approximately twice the size of the church above. Parts of it were filled with soil. Parts were intact. The imaging suggested multiple chambers, all connected. Roman construction throughout.

"This is extraordinary," she said, showing Gregory and Ted the results. "We'll need to bring in a proper team. This could take months to excavate properly."

"How long has it been there?" Gregory asked.

"The construction style suggests the late Roman period. Possibly military. First or second century. And the site..." She gestured at the imaging. "The ground itself shows signs of pre-Roman use. This was sacred ground before the Romans arrived."

Ted made careful notes. Gregory just stared at the scan.

Three religions deep. Just as Carey had said.

The excavation didn't begin immediately. Permits. Planning. Coordination with the Diocese. The church continued its work. Gregory's services. Ted's Thursdays. Margaret's roses.

But word had spread. The paper had been picked up by larger outlets. Roman structure beneath medieval church. Pre-Roman sacred site. The story had a certain appeal.

Which was why, three weeks after the article appeared, someone came to visit.

Late afternoon. The light slanted through the windows the way it did in summer. Gregory was in the vestry when he heard the knock.

A young man stood at the door. Early twenties. Dark sunglasses despite the hour. Polite. Composed.

"I'm sorry to disturb you," he said. "I read about the cellar discovery in the paper. I wondered if I might have a look."

"The excavation hasn't begun yet," Gregory said. "We're waiting on the proper team."

"Of course. I just... I was passing through the area. Thought I'd stop by." He stepped inside and removed his sunglasses. His eyes adjusted to the dimmer light immediately. He inhaled, testing the air, and Gregory saw him pause. Process. "So you're the one they've been talking about."

Gregory felt the recognition settle between them. The scent. The stillness. The particular quality of the air when two vampires occupied the same space.

"And you are?" Gregory asked.

"My name is Pseudolus. I am seventeen hundred years old. But please, call me Phil." He looked around the church with something like affection. "I read about the cellar in the paper. Thought I'd come have a look." A pause. "I was here when they built the bloody thing."

Gregory considered this. For two thousand years, Carey had been alive. This young man -- Phil -- could be any age at all. Seventeen hundred years. Only three hundred years younger than Carey.

Ted is going to be jealous, Gregory thought.

***

Chapter XI -- Kataluma

"And ye shall say unto the goodman of the house, The Master saith unto thee, Where is the guest chamber, where I shall eat the passover with my disciples?" -- Luke 22:11

Phil stayed.

Not in the obvious way -- no announcement, no formal arrangement. He simply appeared most days, usually late morning after the sun had lost its early edge. Sometimes he helped Ted with the restoration work. Sometimes he sat in the nave, perfectly still for hours, just… being there. Gregory found his presence oddly comforting. Ancient and young at the same time. Patient in a way that only came from having seventeen centuries to practice.

The archaeological team arrived three weeks after the initial GPR survey. Five people, led by Dr Alice Wilkins, a woman in her forties with practical boots and a manner that suggested she'd spent more time in muddy trenches than university offices. She set up a small site office in what had been the old choir room, spread her imaging results across the table, and got to work.

Phil appeared on her second day.

"Dr Wilkins," he said, polite as anything. "I wondered if I might ask a favour."

She looked up from her laptop. A young man, early twenties, with the sort of presence that suggested he spent a great deal of time in libraries. "How can I help you?"

"I've been studying the site," Phil said. "Local history enthusiast. The graveyard -- I was wondering if you might have time to run your equipment over it."

"We're here for the Roman structure," Alice said. "Graveyard's not in our remit."

"I understand. But based on the age of the graveyard and the surrounding area, I have a high belief that the people buried there have decomposed back to organic matter.

The marsh soil conditions..." He trailed off. "It would be useful to confirm. If you had a spare afternoon."

Alice studied him. The way he talked about soil chemistry, decomposition rates -- this wasn't casual interest. This was someone who'd done the reading. "You've studied the period extensively."

"I find it fascinating," Phil said.

She smiled slightly. There was something about him. An old soul, she thought. The kind of person who seemed to carry more than their years. "All right. Thursday afternoon. We'll have a look." "Thank you."

They did it on a Thursday, whilst Ted was on his blood run. Phil stood at the edge of the graveyard, watching the equipment operator move methodically across the consecrated ground. Alice came to stand beside him.

"You were right," she said, spreading the imaging across the bonnet of her Land Rover. "Look."

The graveyard showed clear signs of disturbance -- graves had been dug here, no question. Rectangular depressions in the soil. Patterns of fill. But no solid remains. No bones. No coffins. Just... earth.

"The marsh," Alice said. "Wet, acidic soil. Organic material doesn't last. Everything's turned to dust." She traced one of the rectangular shapes. "People were buried here, probably for centuries. But there's nothing left to find."

"And no Roman structure underneath?" Phil asked.

"Nothing. The cellar system doesn't extend this far." She looked at him with something like respect. "You have a real feel for this period. It's almost like you lived in it."

Phil smiled. "I've always found Roman construction methods interesting." "Well, your hypothesis was spot-on. Good work."

What she didn't know: he'd watched people get buried in that graveyard for over a thousand years. Knew exactly what the marsh would do to their remains. Knew every inch of what lay beneath because he'd built the structure that didn't extend there.

What he didn't say: it would make a very nice place for a kip.

Ted found Phil in the graveyard that evening, standing among the headstones as the light faded.

"Alice showed me the imaging," Ted said.

"Did she?"

"No bodies. Just dust. You knew that already."

Phil turned to look at him. "Seventeen hundred years. I've watched every burial. Knew what the soil would do."

"You're thinking it's a good place to rest."

Phil smiled. "Consecrated ground. Peaceful. No awkward discoveries if someone digs. Yes. It would suit."

"Right then." Ted made a note in his book. "I'll have a word with the Diocese. Markers need relocating anyway -- respectful thing to do, given there's nothing underneath them anymore. Once that's sorted, we could make it a contemplation garden. A place for people to sit. Think about God. That sort of thing."

"Thank you, Ted."

"Might as well," Ted said. "Nothing else pressing on."

***

The Diocese approved the graveyard transformation with surprising speed. The 1611 Bible had provided more than enough funds for both the parking expansion and the garden project. Markers would be carefully relocated to a memorial wall. The ground itself would be cleared, planted with native marsh grasses, and a few benches would be installed. A place of quiet reflection. Pastoral care.

Ted presented it to Gregory as a fait accompli one Tuesday morning.

"Thought it might be nice," Ted said. "Give visitors somewhere to sit. Bit of peace."

Gregory looked at the plans. Simple. Tasteful. Practical. "It's a lovely idea, Ted."

"Diocese is keen. Funds are there. Just need your blessing."

Gregory signed the approval without hesitation. A contemplation garden. A place of rest. It seemed entirely appropriate.

Ted folded the papers carefully. "Phil may nap in it from time to time."

Gregory smiled. "I imagine he might."

The village's response to the discovery was measured but real. Appledore, three miles down the road, found its pub suddenly busier. The Black Lion started serving lunch six days a week instead of four. The tea room extended its hours. A small bed-and-breakfast that had been thinking about closing decided to stay open after all.

Brookland, closer to Fairfield, saw the occasional archaeologist stopping to admire St Augustine's famous detached bell tower. The village shop sold more bottled water and sandwiches than it had in years.

At St Thomas à Becket itself, Sunday attendance crept upward. Not dramatically. But where there had been eight or nine parishioners, now there were twelve. Then fifteen. Curious visitors who'd read about the discovery in the paper came to see the church and stayed for the service. Some came back the following week.

Gregory found himself preparing sermons for an audience that wasn't entirely familiar anymore. He kept his words simple. Clear. Welcoming. Making room.

The kitchen smelled of cinnamon. Gregory found Abigail's pie on the counter, still warm beneath its cloth covering. She'd been doing this for months now -- arriving quietly, leaving something warm, gone before he could thank her. Apple and cinnamon this time.

This time, she was still there, tidying the kitchen, when Gregory returned from speaking with Alice about the week's excavation schedule.

"Abigail," he said. "Thank you. It smells wonderful."

She smiled, wiping her hands on her apron. "Thought you might like something warm. Nothing better than warm pie on a summer afternoon."

"My diet doesn't really allow for it anymore," Gregory said. "But would you mind if I gave it to Ted? He's been working so hard on the restoration."

"Of course, Father. Whatever you think best."

They stood there for a moment, the pie between them, and Gregory caught the scent. Not cinnamon. Not Apple. Something sharp underneath. Ammonia. Like a litter box that needed changing.

Not on her hands. On her. Coming from her skin, her breath, the air around her.

Uremic smell. Kidney failure.

Gregory kept his expression neutral, his voice gentle. "How long has it been since you've seen Dr Patel?"

She smiled, wiping her hands on her apron. "Oh, years now, Father. I don't much care for doctors."

"Would you do me a favour and make a visit? Just routine."

She paused. Then, quietly: "Trust in the Lord with all thine heart; and lean not unto thine own understanding."

Gregory waited.

She smiled. "All right, Father. I'll make an appointment."

"Thank you, Abigail."

After she left, Gregory picked up the phone and called Ted. "When you come by later, there's a pie in the kitchen. Abigail made it. Apple and cinnamon."

"Right then," Ted said. "The missus will be pleased."

Gregory hung up and stood in the nave for a long moment. The church was quiet. Light slanting through the windows.

***

Phil appeared in the doorway, backlit by the late afternoon sun.

"The garden's coming along," he said. "Ted's doing good work."

"He always does."

Phil walked into the nave, his footsteps quiet on the stone floor. "Building a guest chamber, aren't you? For all of us. The living. The dead. The in-between."

Gregory looked at him. "Am I?"

"I think so," Phil said. "You just never anticipated how many guests you're expecting yet."

In the kitchen, Abigail's pie sat cooling on the counter. In the graveyard, benches were being installed among the marsh grass. In Appledore, the pub was setting extra tables. In the church itself, the pews waited for Sunday's larger congregation.

And underneath it all, seventeen hundred years of Roman stonework, built by a young man who was still here, still watching, still helping tend the space he'd made so long ago.

Kataluma. The guest chamber.

They were building it together.

***

Chapter XII -- The Foundation

"To receive the instruction of wisdom, justice, and judgment, and equity; To give subtilty to the simple, to the young man knowledge and discretion." -- Proverbs 1:2–4

It happened during the Thursday sermon.

Gregory was midway through his homily on Proverbs -- instruction, understanding, the fear of the Lord -- when he heard it. Not with his ears. Deeper than that. A rhythm that didn't belong.

Thump thump thump THUMP.

A man in the third row. Guest parishioner, visiting from Brookland. His heart was beating against his chest like it was trying to escape. Irregular. Wrong. Dangerous.

Gregory stopped mid-sentence. "Ted, could you come here a moment?"

Ted rose from his seat at the side and came to the pulpit.

Gregory leaned close, whispered, "Third row. Heart. Call an ambulance. Now."

Ted nodded once. Quiet. Slipped out through the vestry door.

Gregory returned to his sermon. "The fear of the Lord is the beginning of knowledge..." His voice was steady. The congregation didn't notice the pause. Or if they did, they thought nothing of it.

Five minutes later, Ted returned. Took his seat. Nodded again.

Gregory continued preaching.

Ten minutes after that, there was movement at the back. Two paramedics, quiet, professional, slipping in through the rear entrance. They positioned themselves in the vestry doorway. Waited.

The man in the third row clutched his chest. Made a small sound. Slumped forward.

The medics were already moving. Equipment out. Responding. The congregation barely had time to register what was happening before the man was being stabilised, assessed, and prepared for transport.

"How did you--" someone started to ask.

But there was no answer. Just Gregory, standing at the pulpit, watching the medics work. Just Ted, notebook already out, ready to call the man's family.

The medics saved him. Heart attack, they said later. Caught early. Good timing. Lucky.

"Divine intervention," someone said in the car park afterward.

The story spread.

***

The Diocese heard about it three days later.

Not just the heart attack. Everything. The archaeological discovery that made the papers. The sudden increase in attendance. The 1611 Bible find. The media attention on a tiny church in the middle of Romney Marsh that nobody had thought about in decades.

And now this. Impossible timing. Medics on scene before the cardiac event. How did Father Chadwick know?

The Bishop's office made a phone call.

"Send someone," they said. "Just to have a look. See what's happening there."

They sent Markus.

***

Markus arrived on a Tuesday, mid-morning, with a clipboard and a brief.

Anglo. Mid-thirties. Possessed of the particular weariness that came from spending a decade watching the Church of England operate from the inside. He knew where the bodies were buried. And the priests relocated.

He'd been sent to assess. Document. Report back. Standard procedure for unusual activity in a parish. Tick the boxes. File the paperwork. Move on.

But Markus had stopped believing in standard procedure around the same time he'd stopped believing the institution he served bore much resemblance to the faith it claimed to represent.

He admired the Jesuits. Their intellectual rigour. Their willingness to sit with complexity. Teilhard de Chardin -- evolution and Christ, science and faith, holding both without flinching. Nobody in the Diocese had ever said that name out loud. Not approvingly.

Markus parked his car in the newly expanded car park -- funded by a 1611 Bible, apparently, which was itself remarkable -- and walked across the footbridge to the church. Water everywhere. Marsh grass. The smell of wet earth and old stone. The smell of sheep gathered everywhere -- he thought about the two flocks, the one outside in the sun, and inside in the church.

St Thomas à Becket stood quietly in the afternoon light. He went inside.

Gregory found him three hours later, sitting in the newly discovered confessional chamber with a toothbrush and a toothpick, carefully cleaning centuries of grime from the Roman carvings.

"I'm sorry," Markus said, not looking up. "I should have asked permission. But I couldn't… I couldn't leave it like this."

The stone was revealing itself. Intricate work. Roman craftsmanship. Sacred space that had stood for seventeen hundred years, waiting for someone to care enough to clean it properly.

Scattered papers on the floor beside him. A piece of charcoal. Markus had made several stone rubbings before starting his cleaning process.

Gregory watched him work. "Take your time," he said.

Markus looked up. "You're Father Chadwick."

"Gregory."

"Markus. Diocese sent me."

"I gathered."

They sat in silence for a moment. Markus returned to his work. Gregory didn't ask about the clipboard. Markus didn't mention his brief.

"This was a confessional," Markus said eventually. "Before it was Christian. Look at the carvings. Multiple deities. This was where Romans came to… what? Confess? Pray? Seek absolution from gods we don't even remember?"

Gregory considered this. "Same human need. Different names for the divine."

Markus smiled slightly. "You sound like a Jesuit."

"I'll take that as a compliment."

A voice from the doorway: "How many different gods did how many Romans confess to?"

They both turned. A young man, early twenties, standing in the entrance to the chamber. Polite. Composed. Watching Markus work with something like approval.

"Phil," Gregory said. "This is Markus. Diocese."

"Phil," the young man said, offering his hand. "Local history enthusiast."

Markus shook it. "That's a good question. I don't know if we'll ever know the answer."

Phil smiled. "No. I suppose we won't."

The excavation had progressed significantly in the weeks since the initial discovery. Lights had been rigged throughout the cellar system. Proper access established. Alice Wilkins' team was working methodically through the chambers, documenting everything.

She invited Phil down on a Thursday afternoon.

"Want to see what we've found?" she asked. "Your insights have been invaluable up top. Thought you might enjoy seeing the rest."

Phil accepted with the easy grace of someone who'd been waiting for the invitation.

They descended together. The air changed as they went deeper. Cooler. Older. The smell of stone and earth and time. Alice's torch beam caught inscriptions on the walls, faded but still visible after seventeen centuries.

She pulled out her phone to translate one. The signal was weak this far down. The app loaded slowly.

"That one says Mithras," Phil said, reading over her shoulder.

Alice looked at the inscription. Looked at her phone. Looked at Phil. "How did you--"

"Studied Latin extensively," Phil said.

She tried the app again. It finally loaded. Mithras.

"Fascinating," she said.

"I studied Latin for three years in university, Sanskrit, hieroglyphics, but your recall and speed is impressive"

They went deeper. More inscriptions. Alice's phone became useless. The signal cut out entirely. She started to ask Phil.

He translated instantly. Every time. Perfectly.

"Dedicated to the unconquered sun."

"Built in the reign of Hadrian."

"This marks the eastern boundary."

Alice stopped pulling out her phone. Just asked. Phil answered. It was faster. More accurate.

They found a channel cut into the stone floor. Water was still running through it. An underground stream. Still functioning. Thousands of years later. Alice knelt, examining the engineering.

"Oh," Phil said. "That was the Roman latrine."

Alice went very still. Looked up at him. "How could you possibly--"

Phil shrugged. "The engineering. Water flow. Drainage. It's quite elegant, really."

Alice stood. Stared at him. "Your instincts are uncanny."

"I've always found Roman construction methods interesting."

She studied him in the torchlight. This young man, who read ancient Latin faster than her translation software. Who knew where the latrine would be before she'd even examined the drainage system? Who moved through these chambers like he'd seen them before.

"Phil," she said carefully. "You're invaluable here. I could get you a position. My team. University funding. You'd be brilliant."

Phil smiled. "I appreciate that. Truly. But I'm still young. I want to explore the world a bit before settling down."

Alice heard: typical early twenties response. Reasonable. Understandable.

What she didn't hear: the weight of seventeen hundred years in the phrase "still young."

Phil found Ted in the contemplation garden that evening. The benches had been installed. Native grasses planted. Peaceful.

"How are the chambers?" Ted asked.

Phil sat down. Laughed. "You won't believe it. They found the brook today -- the latrine system. I said, 'Oh, that was the Roman latrine.' The doctor almost passed out. It was like her head would implode. I fought from laughing."

Ted smiled. "Bet you wanted to tell her you helped build it."

"Every bloody second." Phil shook his head. "And the inscriptions. Ted. The inscriptions."

"What about them?"

"They used Carpi slaves. From the Carpathian region. The walls are loaded with curses and nastiness toward the Romans. Those daft idiots never understood. They thought them history. All they were was Carpi graffiti."

Ted raised his eyebrows. "What sort of graffiti?"

Phil grinned. "'For I would have been your father, but the feral dog was first in her bedchambers.' That's carved into what Alice thinks is a family dedication."

Ted laughed outright.

"And I had to make up bloody gods they were praying to on the walls," Phil continued. "The Romans would ask what the inscriptions meant. I'd tell them -- oh, that's a prayer to the god of cows. That one? Dog deity. There's a god of a vagabond peeing on a wall."

"You're joking."

"I am not. Praise the great goddess Cloacina, goddess of the Cloaca Maxima, queen of the sewer systems. They had us worship the bloody toilet goddess whilst building their empire, and seventeen hundred years later, scholars are writing papers about syncretism."

Ted shook his head, smiling. "You saved them. The slaves. By making up gods."

"Kept them from getting punished for the insults, at least." Phil was quiet for a moment. "I'd forgotten how bad it was. How much we needed the humor. Reading it all again today…"

"Hard?"

"Yes."

***

The next time Alice took Phil into the chambers, they found a particularly long inscription. Multiple lines. Elaborate. Alice shone her torch on it.

"This looks significant," she said. "Can you--"

Phil started reading. Got three words in. Stopped.

It was one of the worst ones. A curse so elaborate, so creative, so absolutely filthy that the Carpi slave who'd carved it must have spent hours getting it right. Phil remembered him. Remembered laughing. Remembered the quiet satisfaction when the Roman overseer had walked past it, nodding approvingly at the 'devotional text.'

Phil started laughing. Couldn't stop. It got worse. The memories flooding back -- the conditions, the anger, the only weapon they'd had being language the Romans couldn't understand. All of it carved into the walls they were forced to build.

He tried to turn the laugh into something else. Failed. His shoulders shook. He covered his face.

Alice put a hand on his shoulder. "Phil?"

He nodded, still covering his face. Trying to compose himself. The laughter was threatening to break through again.

"You're so affected by their history," Alice said softly. "Their suffering. I understand. This kind of work… it gets to you."

Phil managed a breath. Lowered his hands carefully. "Sorry," he said, voice rough.

"Don't be," Alice said. "It means you care."

Yes. That was it. He cared.

That was why he was laughing until his shoulders shook.

***

Markus sat in the vestry that night, long after everyone else had gone home. His official notebook lay closed on the table. Beside it, a different notebook. Smaller. Personal.

He opened it. Wrote the date. Stared at the page.

The brief from the Diocese asked him to assess: unusual activity, financial irregularities, and unexplained phenomena. Tick the boxes. File the report.

He picked up his pen.

What could he possibly write?

Father Chadwick heard a heart attack before it happened. The church has a seventeen-hundred-year-old Roman cellar system built by slaves who spent their captivity carving insults that the Romans couldn't read. A young man who appears to be twenty-three reads ancient Latin like a native speaker and knows where the latrines are without looking.

Markus set down his pen. Made tea. Third cup tonight.

Started again.

The official notebook would say what it needed to say. Standard observations. Nothing concerning. Recommend continued monitoring.

This notebook -- the secret one -- would say what was actually happening.

He just needed to figure out what that was first.

***

Chapter XIII — The Rosetta

"But when he, the Spirit of truth, comes, he will guide you into all the truth. He will not speak on his own; he will speak only what he hears, and he will tell you what is yet to come." -- John 16:13

The email arrived on a Tuesday morning.

Dr. Sarah Okonkwo had been running her haematology practice in South London for fifteen years. Good work. Important work. The kind that saved lives without making headlines. Her equipment was functional, her staff competent, her results solid.

She almost deleted the message. Spam filters usually catch recruitment emails.

Then she saw the name of the sender.

Dr. Sharon Hale.

Sarah sat back in her chair. Nobel Prize. Haematology. Published extensively. One of the most respected researchers in the field. Not spam. Real.

She read the email properly.

Subject: Research Opportunity -- Plasma Institute, London.

The third paragraph mentioned a stipend that made her read it twice more.

She picked up the phone.

The Plasma Institute occupied a converted industrial building in Chelsea. From the outside, unremarkable. Sarah took the Tube from her practice, emerged into the London drizzle, and found the address.

Inside was something else entirely.

Dr. Hale met her in the lobby. Fifties, practical handshake, no small talk. "This way."

They walked through corridors lined with framed photographs and certificates. The Institute's history, displayed chronologically.

1948: A grainy black-and-white photograph. Two men in a warehouse, standing beside what looked like a modified centrifuge. The plaque read: "Founder's son, Kushim Arit II, with first equipment -- centrifuge adapted from milk pasteurization technology."

1956: "Breakthrough in mercury removal from curative treatments." A published paper, framed. Sarah paused. Mercury had been standard practice for decades. Removing it had saved thousands from toxic side effects.

1967: The first proper laboratory. Still modest but growing.

1973: "Advances in sickle cell treatment protocols." Another major journal publication.

1989: International recognition. An award from the World Health Organization.

2003: "Hemophilia Factor VIII synthesis breakthrough." Patent donated to the public domain.

2015: Expansion into rare blood disorder research.

Eighty years of documented medical advancement, traced in photographs, patents, and peer-reviewed publications.

"We started small," Dr. Hale said, not slowing her pace. "Two rooms. Best equipment available at the time. Our first centrifuge was used for pasteurizing milk. Hand cranked. But we had something nobody else did."

"What was that?"

"Time."

They reached a secure door. Dr. Hale scanned her badge. "The founder believed medical knowledge should be shared. We sell equipment we invent and modify to competitors at cost. Publish everything. No patents held for profit."

"That's… unusual."

"Kushim Arit the Fourth gave a speech at our last expansion. He said the same thing his great-grandfather said in 1948: 'This is about saving people, not saving money.'"

The door opened.

Sarah stopped.

Electronic microscopes that cost well over two million euros. Sequencing equipment she'd only seen in journals. Climate-controlled research bays. Fifty-inch LED panels displaying rotating molecular structures, controlled by researchers with iPads. Clean rooms. Staff moving with quiet efficiency.

Her entire practice couldn't afford one piece of this equipment.

"Jesus," she said quietly.

"We take the work seriously," Dr. Hale said. "Because the work matters."

***

The project briefing came that afternoon.

Dr. Hale stood before two LED panels in the conference room. Cellular data rotated in three dimensions. She controlled the display with an iPad, swiping through protein markers, blood work analyses, and molecular structures.

"We've been working on this for three years," she said. "Stuck at the same point the entire time."

Sarah leaned forward, studying the images. Recognition clicked immediately. "Hematotropic pathogen. Protein-mediated binding to host cells."

Dr. Hale looked up. "You've seen this before."

"I have a patient with this condition. I've been examining it for months. But with basic equipment. Standard microscopy." Sarah gestured at the panels. "I've been looking at this with a penlight. You're using Wembley."

Dr. Hale smiled slightly. "Then you understand the problem."

"The pathogen integrates with host cells. It doesn't destroy them -- it rewrites their function. And once integration is complete, it's indistinguishable from normal cellular processes." Dr. Hale pulled up images of failed treatments. "Nothing to target. Nothing to separate. Attempting removal causes immediate systemic failure."

"So it's irreversible."

"In fully integrated subjects, yes." Dr. Hale paused. "We've tried everything. The pathogen is too deeply embedded. Thousands of cases. Globally. Some for… decades. It's a wonder how they still function, but they do."

Sarah said nothing. Decades. Dr. Hale thought decades.

The actual number was centuries. Millennia, in some cases.

But Sarah couldn't say that.

"How many subjects?"

"Thousands. The family of Kushim Arit spent decades building the patient registry. Personal outreach. International travel. Finding cases, earning trust. When someone at their level commits that amount of time…" Dr. Hale shook her head. "You don't see that dedication anymore."

Dr. Hale met her eyes. "It was irreversible. Until you sent us the bloodwork on your patient."

***

Dr. Hale took her to the storage facility that afternoon.

A climate-controlled vault. Vault doors. Digital readouts showing temperature precise to one-tenth of a degree. Radiation shielding. Row after row of preserved samples in perfect stasis.

"We require fresh samples weekly," Dr. Hale explained. RNA degrades within hours. Frozen samples lose integrity. And we need living immune cells for antibody development." She gestured to one section. "But we preserve everything. Perfect conditions. No deviations." Sarah saw the labels. GC-447. Week after week. Months of samples.

"Your patient has been very consistent," Dr. Hale said.

Sarah thought about the weekly trips. The patient traveling from Romney Marsh to London. The routine they'd established. The discipline required to maintain his transitional state.

"He understands what's at stake," Sarah said carefully.

"Does he know what you're working on?"

"He knows we're trying to help. That's enough."

The sample arrived on a Thursday morning.

Fresh draw. GC-447. Sarah ran the initial work-up herself.

But this time, she had access to equipment that cost more than her annual budget.

The electron microscope offered magnification she'd only read about in journals. Six thousand times normal vision. Cellular structures, frozen in extraordinary detail.

Sarah positioned the sample. Adjusted the focus.

Watched.

White blood cells. Leukocytes. And there the pathogen. Inside the cells. At the membrane. Attempting to integrate with cellular machinery.

Contact.

The pathogen's surface proteins reached for binding sites.

Failed.

Another frame. Another attempt.

Failed.

Like a mouse trying to climb a slippery wall. Over and over. Unable to gain purchase.

The pathogen was there. Active. Attempting integration.

But it couldn't hold.

"Like managing HIV," Dr. Hale said quietly. "Present. But controlled."

Sarah pulled up a comparison sample. Normal infection. Standard presentation.

Same pathogen. Same white blood cells.

Contact.

Binding successful. Immediate. The pathogen's proteins locked into place. Integration began.

She switched back to GC-447.

Trying. Failing. Trying. Failing.

The binding sites were exposed. Visible. Distinct from host tissue.

Unattached.

Targetable.

Sarah called Dr. Hale immediately.

They stood together in the empty lab. Two in the morning. Dr. Hale had arrived twenty minutes after Sarah's call, drinking very strong coffee.

"Show me," she said.

Sarah pulled up the microscope feed. "Watch the binding attempts."

Dr. Hale leaned closer. Watched the pathogen try and fail, try and fail. "It can't integrate."

"No. Something's preventing it." Sarah pulled up the patient's medical history. "The diet I prescribed. Controlled blood consumption. Specific iron levels."

"How did you know it would work?"

Sarah shook her head. "I didn't. He told me he was consuming blood. I was just… managing it medically. Controlling his iron levels to prevent toxicity. I wasn't trying to stop the infection. I was trying to keep him safe while he adjusted."

"And it worked."

"Yes. But I didn't know it would." Sarah highlighted the cellular structure. "The iron levels in his bloodstream -- in an ordinary patient, under normal conditions, this would be toxic. But in this unique case, the excess iron isn't strengthening the cells. It's altering the surface chemistry. The receptor conformation. The pathogen can't bind because the attachment sites have changed."

"Like managing HIV," Dr. Hale said quietly. "The virus is present but suppressed."

"Exactly. If he maintains the diet, the iron keeps changing the binding environment. The pathogen can't progress." Sarah paused. "There was some contamination in the first few weeks. Before we established the iron protocol. The pathogen did integrate with some cells. That's why he has… symptoms. But once we got his iron levels right, further integration stopped."

Dr. Hale stared at the screen. "So he's stuck in between. Partially integrated but stable."

"Yes."

Dr. Hale pointed at the exposed binding sites. "And those surface proteins. In fully integrated subjects, they're indistinguishable from host tissue. We can't target them."

"But in GC-447, they're visible. Unattached."

"We can sequence them," Dr. Hale said. "Isolate the pathogen's genome. Map the protein expression. Once we know which proteins it produces…"

"We can design antibodies to target those specific markers," Sarah finished.

They worked for six weeks.

Sequencing the pathogen's genome using Whole Genome Sequencing. Mapping its protein structures, modeling likely conformations with tools like AlphaFold. Identifying pathogen-specific surface markers, then designing monoclonal antibodies to target them. Running computational simulations to test binding efficiency and specificity, iterating through thousands of candidates. Validating targets through proteomic analysis.

Sarah stopped going home. The Institute had a break room with a sofa. Coffee that never ran out. And the singular focus of something that mattered more than sleep.

"We weren't starting from zero," Dr. Hale said one night, eyes on the simulation results. "We had three years of failed attempts. Thousands of samples. We just didn't know what we were looking at."

The simulations were resolved on a Saturday morning. Perfect antibody binding. The pathogen's exposed protein markers were neutralized. Immune system clearance projected at ninety-eight percent.

Dr. Hale stared at the screen. "We need to test it."

"In vitro first," Sarah said. "Not on the patient. Not yet."

Dr. Hale nodded. "Agreed."

They scheduled the test for the following Thursday.

Fresh sample. GC-447. Morning draw.

Sarah prepared the antibody solution herself. Monoclonal antibodies suspended in saline. Clear. Colorless. Unremarkable.

Everything they'd worked for, contained in ten milliliters.

Under the electron microscope at six thousand times magnification, they watched.

The enriched immune environment. Active white blood cells. Natural killer cells. The antibodies entering the sample.

Finding the pathogen.

Binding to the pathogen-specific surface proteins -- both the unattached attempts and the successfully integrated contamination from those first two weeks.

The protein markers were recognized. Targeted. Neutralized.

And then -- slowly, methodically -- the immune system moved in. White blood cells engulfed the now-visible pathogen. Cleared it.

All of it. Integrated and unintegrated.

Ten minutes later, Sarah ran a clean scan.

Normal white blood cells. Healthy. Functioning.

No pathogen.

No infection.

Just clean blood.

Dr. Hale exhaled. "It worked."

Sarah couldn't speak yet. She ran the test again. Same result. Again. Same result.

The cure existed.

They ran projections that evening. What would happen in fully integrated subjects.

The antibodies would still work. Still recognize the pathogen-specific proteins. Still neutralize and clear.

But the outcome would be different.

"In full integration," Sarah explained, pulling up the models, "the pathogen isn't just attached. It's maintaining essential cellular functions. Repair mechanisms. Metabolic processes. Everything."

Dr. Hale nodded slowly. "So when it's removed--"

"The body doesn't age," Sarah said quietly. "It fails. The pathogen has been maintaining systems that can no longer function independently. Without it, there's nothing left to sustain basic cellular processes."

"How quickly?"

Sarah showed her the timeline. "Moments. Catastrophic system collapse. The cells revert briefly to their unmodified state, but they can't maintain themselves. Immediate organ failure."

Dr. Hale was quiet. "Would they feel it?"

"Briefly. Maybe twenty, thirty seconds of being free of infection. Normal sensation. Then the systems fail."

"Painful?"

"Should be quick enough that awareness doesn't last long enough for pain. Just… sudden biological shutdown."

Dr. Hale stared at the data. "So for your patient, this is a cure. For older patients…"

Sarah met her eyes. "It's terminal. But peaceful. Chosen."

They sat in silence.

"For patients like GC-447," Dr. Hale said finally, "caught in transition, pathogen partially integrated -- this is complete removal. Actual cure."

"Yes."

"And for fully integrated subjects…"

Sarah thought: Choice. Finally. After centuries.

But she said, "They would have options. For the first time. Live with the infection or terminate."

***

Sarah found Dr. Hale in her office the next day.

"We should tell your patient," Dr. Hale said. "GC-447. The treatment is proven. We can offer it."

"I will," Sarah said. She sat down. "But there's something else."

Dr. Hale waited.

"I have another patient. Fully integrated presentation. They've had the condition for… a very long time. They understand what the treatment would mean. The outcome."

"And they want it anyway."

"Yes. But they need time first. To get their affairs in order." Sarah met her eyes. "They want me to administer the treatment. At their home. They feel safe with me. Only me in attendance."

Dr. Hale was quiet for a moment. "How long do they need?"

"A few weeks. Maybe a month."

"You'll let me know when it's time?"

"Of course."

Silence settled between them. Sarah could see Dr. Hale processing what she'd just agreed to -- a treatment that would end someone's life. Administered in their home. By choice.

Dr. Hale stood. Walked to the window. When she spoke again, her voice was different. Quieter.

"This work we've done. It matters."

She turned back. "If this mechanism works -- targeting persistent pathogen integration based on protein mapping -- we might be able to apply it to rabies. Other blood-borne infections. And we've observed the pathogen's regenerative properties at the wound site. If we could isolate that mechanism without the systemic integration… burn treatment, surgical recovery, trauma care." Her eyes were bright. "Sometimes the greatest medical breakthroughs come from unexpected places. Research into one condition reveals principles that transform how we treat dozens of others."

Sarah watched her. This was why scientists lived for this. The possibility. The what if. The door opens onto something that could change everything.

Dr. Hale saw a medical breakthrough that could save countless human lives.

Sarah saw vampires finally being offered choice.

Both were right.

Dr. Hale looked at the data one more time. Smiled slightly.

"The Iron Shield. That's what we should call it."

***

Chapter XIV — The Proceeding

*"Set your house in order, for you shall die; you shall not recover." -- 2
Kings 20:1*

Umbra sat on her couch, stroking her cat, Familiar. The black cat purred under her hand, eyes half-closed in contentment. The telly played in the background, some documentary she wasn't watching.

Her phone pinged.

She glanced at the screen.

Message from Dr. Sharon Hale: "Cure located and tested."

Umbra smiled, nodding.

"This will make someone very happy," she said to Familiar.

She picked up her phone. She dialed.

Carey answered on the second ring.

"They've done it," Umbra said.

A beat.

Carey grinned widely. She could hear it in his voice.

"About bloody time."

They both started laughing.

The laughter went on for several seconds -- relief, joy, disbelief after so many years of waiting. Finally, Carey caught his breath.

"I have so much to do," he said, almost sarcastically, still laughing. "And so little time."

Umbra snorted. "Yes. Time. Such a bother."

More laughter.

Then Carey cleared his throat.

"Monday evening. Executive meeting at the offices. Everyone concerned, including the true vampires -- the lawyers."

Umbra chortled. "This is not how I anticipated this call would go. I am truly happy for you, sir."

A pause. Warmth in his voice.

"Thank you, Umbra."

He rang off.

Umbra sat there, smiling. Familiar rubbed against her, purring.

She stroked his head.

"Someone is going home," she said to the cat.

***

Gregory sat at his desk, writing his sermon for Sunday. The afternoon light slanted through the window, casting long shadows across the page.

A knock at the door.

Ted popped his head in. "You have a visitor. Don't need the rosaries."

Sarah Okonkwo walked in behind him. She had the biggest smile.

"Thanks, Ted," she said.

Gregory looked up. "Can we have a moment?"

Ted nodded and left, closing the door behind him.

Gregory stared at Sarah. She looked terrible. Exhausted. Dark circles under her eyes. Hair pulled back messily. Like she hadn't slept properly in weeks.

He stood, almost horrified.

"Have you been infected by the virus? You look worse than me!"

Sarah laughed. "Well, I have been living a vampire lifestyle for the last six weeks. Living on liquid and sleeping on a couch."

Before Gregory could respond, she blurted out:

"We did it. Found a cure."

Silence.

Gregory stood there, processing.

Then Sarah moved forward and suddenly hugged him.

He stood there, not knowing what to do.

Her scent was strong. He smelled the coffee in her hair. Felt her heart beating rapidly against his chest.

And felt something he hadn't felt in twenty years.

Desire.

It all confused him. The enhanced senses making everything more intense. The warmth of her. The closeness. The vulnerability.

He hugged her back. Then gently pushed her back, creating space.

Her face was full of tears. All her professionalism had evaporated.

He nodded, taking it all in. Guided her to the couch. "Let me make some tea."

He needed a moment.

When he returned with two cups, she had composed herself. She thanked him. Apologized for the outburst. Accepted the tea.

They both held their cups. Gregory didn't drink from his -- he couldn't, the tea would make him sick -- but he held it anyway, being proper.

Sarah sipped hers.

"So your blood was the Rosetta Stone," she said. "They had a thousand samples of vampire blood. The head of the company personally travelled the world getting samples. They've been working on this for three years. Your blood, Gregory. Your blood was the key. It made the difference."

Gregory stared at her. "My blood?"

"Your blood, with the extra iron, acted as a shield." She laughed. "Dr. Hale dubbed the cure 'The Iron Shield.' When the infection tries to take hold and change your cells, it prevents it. The reason you have some… symptoms is that the first few days the infection went unchecked, till we got your diet proper."

Gregory asked quietly, "After applying the cure, do the changes in biology stay?"

Sarah smiled. She shook her head. "No. It reverses the condition completely. There is no leftover component of the infection."

Gregory nodded. Filed it away.

"What about others afflicted with the infection?"

Sarah's face took on a sudden sadness.

"I'm afraid once the infection takes over the body, without it the body can no longer sustain life."

Gregory thought for a moment.

"They now have a choice. Carey calls it the 'yetziat neshamah.'"

"Carey?" Sarah looked confused. "Who is Carey?"

Gregory laughed. "That's Arit. The person who is two thousand years old, who owns the Arit Foundation, who owns and runs the Plasma Institute."

"I thought it was his great-grandson."

Gregory smiled. "No. It's him. The original."

Sarah sat back, processing.

"Ms. Shadows -- she is his person -- phoned me, several weeks ago, told me he has volunteered to be patient zero to test the cure. But at his home."

She sat there, suddenly realizing the scope of it all. And the incredible responsibility.

They both sat in silence.

Outside, sheep were making their own statements on the matter.

Gregory paused. Said quietly:

"My teachings say this is a sin, what he wants. But my brain and heart know it's what he needs. He is a man who made his peace with his Lord a millennium ago. I am not here as judge and jury. You and I are just instruments of the Lord."

Sarah looked at him. "And what about you? What do you need, Gregory?"

He smiled. "Just time."

***

The corporate boardroom occupied the top floor of a glass tower in central London. Floor-to-ceiling windows showed the city spread out below, the Thames winding through it like a silver thread in the late afternoon light.

Eighteen people sat at a long table.

Carey sat at the head, looking polished in casual clothing, as he'd just come from a tennis match. Relaxed. At peace.

The table was a mix of executives, lawyers, accountants, and a few who sat with a certain stillness that marked them as something other than human. The vampires who knew the truth.

Carey looked around the table. Smiled.

"The Foundation, the companies, all of it. Arit Foundation is being restructured. I am, after eighty-one years, retiring. And today, my birthday, is a perfect time to announce it."

The table looked at each other.

The vampires nodded. Knowing.

Lawyers and assistants started typing on laptops.

"The new CEO of the company is Ms. Umbra Shadows. In her years of service, I have never met someone as capable and thoughtful as her to continue my message of world health."

Umbra sat composed, professional. But her eyes showed the weight of what she was inheriting.

"There are a thousand details to be sorted out. If you look at your binders, there is a twenty-three-page document explaining where funding is going, ownership details. All further questions are now addressed by Ms. Shadows."

He paused. Let that settle.

"As far as my plans: there is one place I have desired to visit for a very long time. It is my plan to go there and spend the rest of my days."

You could see how pleased he was. How at peace.

Umbra, shocked but maintaining a professional demeanour, sat straighter.

Carey was truly enjoying this moment.

He was the king of the world.

***

Carey's home was filled with people and laughter.

He moved through the rooms in silk pajamas, playing host, welcoming people warmly. Gregory was there. Sarah. Umbra. Several close vampire friends who'd known him for centuries.

The feeling was almost festive. Not somber. Not tragic.

A celebration.

Conversations drifted through the rooms. Talking about Rome when it fell. The first wars. Spartans. Greek mythology. As well as conversations of banking, equities, and crypto futures.

Ancient and modern mixed seamlessly, because to immortals, it was all recent memory.

Gregory stayed close to Sarah, almost hiding behind her. He felt out of place among these beings who'd lived millennia. She was anchoring him. Sarah was chatting and keeping up with the conversations. Talking about the medical breakthroughs the Foundation had achieved. How this latest cure had the additional possibilities of a rabies cure and rapid skin healing. She fit in naturally, connecting through science and contribution.

The vial sat in a fridge in Carey's bedroom. Waiting.

Carey walked up to Gregory. Clapped a hand on his shoulder.

"Enjoy this moment. When you have lived ten million moments, they blur. I made it my lifetime endeavour to enjoy as many as I can. It's all we have that is our own."

He smiled at Gregory. Then his expression shifted slightly. More serious.

"Before the injection, Father, would you say something? My relationship with the Almighty has been tumultuous at best. When I get up there, I have a few comments I will make, and would like a nice introduction from you."

Gregory smiled.

"I would be honoured. But after all the good you've done, it may run a few hours."

They both laughed. Carey clapped his hands.

"Enough with this dawdling! Let's get on with it!"

It was quiet in his upstairs bedroom. A dramatic king bed, with deep purple velvet.

Under the bed was a platform containing earth -- a tribute to his lifetimes.

Gregory, Umbra, and Sarah were the only three in attendance. This was Carey's request that everyone honoured.

Carey sat on his bed, fluffed up the pillow, and laid back, like he was about to watch a documentary on the migration of sparrows.

Not to end his life.

Gregory spoke.

"People have always considered life as a ledger. The good you have done, the bad, and at the end, where do you end up. I am sure that Kushim Arit has written in both sides of that ledger. And whatever red he had written in the first chapter, he has erased a thousand-fold in the second.

"He was not a human, but humanity was his biggest priority. He never lost his soul and his connection with the Almighty -- no matter what name that entity had at the time."

"I cannot say how many languages Carey has spoken in his life, in his years… but I thought of the ancient Hebrews, and their prayer in the end:

"Sh'ma Yisrael Adonai Eloheinu Adonai Echad."

"Hear, O Israel: The Lord is our God, the Lord is One."

"We don't mourn the end. We celebrate the new beginning."

Gregory looked at Carey. A blood tear in his eye.

"Happy birthday."

Carey smiled. Looked up at him.

"Heghlu'meH QaQ jajvam."

[Today is a good day to die.]

Sarah gently took his arm. He smiled up at her. She injected the serum into it.

After a moment, Carey's face lit up, his cheeks flushed.

"I can feel… warmth…"

"My heart… it's beating… normally…"

"I can breathe…"

A beat.

"This is what it was like…"

Softer:

"I'd forgotten…"

His eyes fluttered for a moment.

He turned to dust.

It settled on the bed -- all that remained were his pajamas, covered in dust.

Then a great thunderclap.

The windows vibrated -- just for a second.

Then absolute silence.

Sarah, who had been weeping softly, looked at Umbra.

"The king is dead… long live the queen."

FOR IMMEDIATE RELEASE

Plasma Institute Announces Successful Development of Iron Shield Treatment Protocol

LONDON, UK — The Plasma Institute, a leader in hematological research and rare blood disorder treatment, announced today the successful completion of clinical testing for Iron Shield, a novel therapeutic intervention for patients suffering from a rare hematotropic pathogen.

The treatment, developed over three years of intensive research, targets a persistent blood-borne infection previously considered irreversible in advanced stages. Iron Shield utilizes monoclonal antibody therapy derived from patient immune profiles to achieve pathogen clearance.

"This represents a significant advancement in our understanding of chronic pathogen integration," said Dr. Sharon Hale, Nobel laureate and lead researcher at the Plasma Institute. "The Iron Shield protocol demonstrates promising applications beyond the immediate patient population."

Initial testing has shown a 98% clearance rate in qualifying patients. The treatment is currently available through specialist consultation for individuals meeting specific diagnostic criteria.

The Plasma Institute has indicated potential future applications of the Iron Shield methodology, including possible interventions for rabies and other persistent viral infections, as well as regenerative medicine applications derived from observed wound-healing properties during the research process.

Founded in 1948, the Plasma Institute has maintained a commitment to advancing global health through accessible medical research. The organization publishes all findings in peer-reviewed journals and provides equipment to research institutions globally at cost.

For more information about Iron Shield or to inquire about patient eligibility, healthcare providers may contact the Plasma Institute directly.

Media Contact: Plasma Institute Communications
press@plasmainstitute.org

Chapter XV — The Incertitude

"Examine yourselves, to see whether you are in the faith. Test yourselves." -- 2 Corinthians 13:5

The car ride from Leeds Castle to St Thomas à Becket was 40 minutes on a good day. Today was a good day. The M20 was clear, the afternoon sun slanting through the beech trees that lined the road, and the town car moved with the particular silence of a vehicle that cost more than most houses.

Gregory sat in the back of the town car. Sarah sat beside him. The privacy screen was up. The driver was just a shape beyond the glass.

They had been quiet since leaving the castle. The gathering had been -- Gregory was not certain what to call it. A celebration. A wake. A farewell to someone who had chosen his own end and done so with grace. Carey's arrangements had been precise. The transportation. The catering. The guest list. Everything handled. Everything considered.

Including, apparently, the ride home.

Sarah broke the silence as they passed the turn for Ashford and the A2070.

"When would you like the injection?"

Gregory looked at her. She was watching her hands. Her jaw was set in the way it got when she was managing something difficult.

He considered the question. Thought about it the way he thought about most things -- carefully, without hurry, until the answer presented itself.

"I don't," he said.

Her hands tightened in her lap. She did not look at him.

"You don't," she repeated.

"No."

A pause. Through the window, a sheep in a field looked up as they passed, chewing steadily, unbothered by the small drama unfolding in the car.

"Don't you want to be cured?" Sarah said. Her voice was careful. Clinical. The voice she used when she was trying very hard not to let her feelings into the room. "Go back to a normal life?"

Gregory smiled. Not unkindly.

"After these ten weeks with this condition," he said quietly, "I have been able to help more people than I ever did when I was just me."

She glanced at him. Back to her hands.

"I hear hummingbirds' heartbeats," Gregory continued. "I can feel God's heartbeat -- in the earth, in the sky. I can smell honeysuckle that's five miles away." He paused. "I can help so many more in this condition. I understand it's a sacrifice on my own life. But I made that choice twenty years ago when I entered the church. To serve others."

Sarah was quiet for a long moment. The car turned onto the smaller road that led towards the marsh. The landscape opened up -- flat, wide, the kind of horizontal that made the sky feel bigger than it had any right to be.

"Gregory," she said finally. "You're choosing to stay infected with a pathogen. Do you understand that? From a medical standpoint, that's -- " She stopped. Started again. "You could be normal again. Fully human. No weekly treatments. No dietary restrictions. No -- "

"No gift of God," Gregory said gently.

She looked at him sharply.

"You used my blood to create the cure," Gregory said. "My blood was the key. The Rosetta Stone, you called it. Don't you see? I was meant to have this. Not to suffer from it. To understand it. To witness what it is. To help those who carry it."

"You're a priest," Sarah said. Her voice was strained now, the clinical veneer cracking. "You could go back to being just a priest. You don't need this to serve God."

"No," Gregory agreed. "I don't need it to serve God. But I need it to serve all."

"All."

"The others. The ones who carry this. Who has carried it for decades. Centuries. Who needs someone who understands. Who can tell them: you are not damned. You are not monsters. You have a condition. And now you have a choice."

The car slowed as they approached the causeway. The church was visible now in the distance, squat and unremarkable, sitting in the marsh the way it had sat there since 1200.

Sarah turned to look at him properly. Her eyes were red.

"I worked myself sick," she said quietly. "Six weeks. Sleeping on a couch. Living on coffee and protein bars. I used your blood -- your blood, Gregory -- to make this cure. And you're saying you don't want it."

Gregory met her gaze.

"I am grateful," he said. "More than I can express. You gave Carey peace. You gave him moments of being human again. Of feeling warmth. Of breathing. You gave him the gift of choosing his own death with dignity. That is -- " He paused. "That is holy work, Sarah. Whether you believe in God or not, what you did is holy."

She was crying. Not dramatically. Just tears, silent, running down her face.

"I wanted to cure you," she said. "I wanted you to be normal again."

"I know."

"I don't want you to suffer."

"I'm not suffering," Gregory said gently. "I promise you. I'm not."

She wiped her eyes with the back of her hand. Took a breath. The professional mask was trying to reassemble itself.

"You'll still need weekly visits," she said. Back to clinical. Back to what she could control. "The blood supplements. The monitoring. If your iron levels spike, we'll need to manage that. And the sensory issues -- if the photophobia worsens, or the enhanced hearing becomes painful -- "

"I understand," Gregory said. "And I'll continue the regiment."

A pause.

"This is mental," Sarah said quietly.

"Perhaps," Gregory said. "But I think -- " He stopped. Started again. "I think Edmund found me for a reason. I think God allowed this to happen because there is work to be done. And I think refusing the cure when so many have suffered without hope of one -- I think that would be the real madness."

The car pulled into the car park. The engine went quiet. The driver remained beyond the glass, giving them privacy.

"Edmund said 'thank you' when he died," Gregory said. "When the cross went into his chest. He looked at me and said Thank you.' I didn't understand it then. I do now."

He reached for the door handle.

"He was seeking what Carey found," Gregory said. "Peace. Release. The end of carrying this burden. And now, because of your work, others can choose that too. Or they can choose to stay. To live with it. To manage it. Either way -- it's a choice. That's what you've given them, Sarah. Not just a cure. A choice."

He opened the door. The marsh air came in -- cold, damp, carrying the smell of watercourses and sheep and the particular green of things that grew in wet places.

"Will you come in for tea?" Gregory asked.

Sarah looked at him. Her eyes were red. Her face was blotchy. She looked, Gregory thought, exactly like someone who had worked herself sick to save someone who did not want to be saved.

She also looked, he thought, beautiful.

He filed that thought away in the part of his mind marked never to be returned to and firmly closed the door on it.

"I should get back to London," Sarah said. "I have -- " She gestured vaguely. "Paperwork. Follow-up. The Foundation will want a full report on Carey's -- " She stopped. "On the procedure."

"Of course."

"Same time next week?" She was back to clinical now. Doctor and patient. Professional boundaries reassembling themselves.

"Same time next week," Gregory confirmed.

He got out of the car. Stood for a moment with his hand on the door.

"Sarah," he said.

She looked up at him.

"Thank you," he said. "For everything. For understanding. For not -- " He paused. "For letting me make my own choice."

She nodded. Did not trust herself to speak.

Gregory closed the door. The car reversed, turned, and headed back down the causeway towards the road. Back to her offices in London. He watched it go the way he always did -- until it disappeared and the only sounds were the watercourses and the sheep and the particular silence that Romney Marsh made when it had the evening to itself.

He stood there for a moment longer.

The honeysuckle was blooming somewhere to the east. Five miles, perhaps six. He could smell it clearly. Could smell the sheep in the next field and the rain coming in off the Channel and the particular scent of the marsh when the tide was turning.

He turned and walked towards the church.

The door was open. It was always open.

He ducked as he went through.

The way you breathe. The way you put the kettle on.

***

Three months had passed since Carey had chosen the 'yetziat neshamah.'

Umbra Shadows sat in what had been his study at Leeds Castle, surrounded by the accumulated detritus of a life that had spanned longer than most civilisations. The mahogany desk in front of her held a laptop, three folders, and a cup of blood tea that had gone cold an hour ago.

She had been working through the inventory for six weeks.

The artwork had been straightforward enough. Renaissance masterpieces -- not acquired, she had learned, but commissioned.

Carey had known da Vinci. Had sat for Raphael. Had walked through studios in Florence when the paint was still wet. Every piece had been donated to the Louvre, as per his instructions. Let the world have them.

All except one.

The portrait hung on the wall behind her now. Kushim Arit, painted by Salvador Mundi sometime in the 1490s. Carey, as he had been five hundred years ago -- the same face, the same eyes, the same particular way he had of looking at the painter as though he could see straight through to whatever came after this.

She had kept that one.

The Rolls-Royce Phantom had been garaged. Umbra preferred her Mercedes SUV, though filling the sixty-litre tank cost over a hundred pounds these days. Vampires are the monsters, she had thought drily, watching the numbers climb at the petrol station.

The Gulfstream G550 had been relocated to Heathrow. Not for luxury -- Umbra had no interest in that -- but because it was practical. She had meetings. Factories to visit. A global operation to run.

Leeds Castle itself she had kept. The Foundation would use it as a remote office. Housing for travelling vampires. "Our dirt is much softer here," she had told the first arrivals, grinning at their bemused faces. Let them think she was joking.

The real work had been the gold.

Ten billion pounds' worth, stored in vaults across three continents. Ancient wealth. Literally. Carey had been accumulating it since before paper money existed.

Umbra had decided to use it to fund a bank. A proper one. Because vampires needed debit cards. Bank accounts. Ways to navigate a world that required proof of identity and employment history, and all the things immortals could not easily provide.

The Vampire Bank. She was still working on the name.

She had purchased a factory near Foyle Food Group in Gloucester. Cow blood processing. She had built a small airstrip nearby so she could fly in for meetings. The Gulfstream was proving useful.

V-Sustenance. The first production run would be ready in six months to a year.

She had started hiring. Vampires, mostly. Old ones who understood discretion. New ones who needed purpose. A company to track, manage, and support. Offer assistance. Counselling. Financial management. Offices in London, Paris, New York, Amsterdam, Bucharest.

She had purchased a logistics company. V-Air. Vampire travel, refrigerated distribution for V-Sustenance. products. Plans to open local factories. Scale the operation.

And she had contacted Sarah.

"Would you be interested in creating a beverage?"

Sarah had the expertise. The team. The Plasma Institute had doctors and scientists doing serious work. Umbra respected that. Respected her.

The laptop screen in front of her now showed a spreadsheet. Assets. Liabilities. Projections. The Foundation was stable. The companies were launching. The infrastructure was being built.

Carey had spent his life trying to cure vampirism.

Umbra was building the infrastructure to live with it.

Her flat in London had not changed. Her life had not changed. She still drove the Mercedes. Still complained about petrol prices. Still lived with Familiar, who had opinions about everything and expressed them at three in the afternoon.

The billions were a tool. Not a lifestyle.

She closed the laptop. Looked at the portrait on the wall.

Kushim Arit. Carey. The man who had built all of this and then chosen to leave it.

Umbra had seen so much death. She had no time to grieve.

But she had kept the portrait.

That would have to be enough.

Chapter XVI — The Consideration

"Rejoice with those who rejoice; mourn with those who mourn." --
Romans 12:15

The three visitors arrived separately but sat together.

Gregory noticed them during the opening hymn -- back pew, left side, the spot where tourists usually sat when they wandered in during services to look at the box pews and take photographs of the triple-decker pulpit. Except that these three were not taking photographs. They were watching him.

Not watching the church. Watching him.

He filed it away and continued the service.

Margaret had chosen "All Things Bright and Beautiful" for the hymn, which was her way of reminding the congregation that spring existed even when February was doing its level best to suggest otherwise. The regulars sang with the particular restraint of Church of England parishioners who had been taught that enthusiasm during worship was vaguely unseemly. The three visitors did not sing. They simply watched.

Gregory delivered his sermon from John 12:40. He had chosen it three days ago, sitting at his desk in the vestry whilst the marsh outside conducted its usual negotiations with the rain.

"He has blinded their eyes and hardened their heart, lest they
see with their eyes, and understand with their heart, and turn, and I
would heal them."

He spoke about seeing without eyes. About understanding without sight. About the ways we perceive truth when the obvious path is closed to us.

The three visitors sat very still.

Gregory understood, somewhere between the second point and the third, exactly what they were. He had been doing this long enough now to recognise the particular quality of attention that vampires brought to a room. They did not fidget. They did not check their phones. They simply listened with the focus of people who had learned, over decades or centuries, that time was the one thing they had in abundance, and rushing through it served no purpose.

He finished the sermon. Led the closing hymn. Gave the benediction.

The congregation filed out the way they always did -- handshakes, brief conversations about the weather, and Mrs. Alderton's niece, who was getting married in May, and whether the leak in the north transept had been properly addressed this time. The three visitors waited until the last of the regulars had gone, then stood as one and walked towards the door.

They did not stop to shake his hand. They simply looked at him -- a long, assessing look -- thanked him, and left.

Verification complete.

Gregory stood at the door and watched them go. They walked down the causeway together, their footsteps synchronised in a way that suggested they had been travelling as a group for some time. When they reached the car park, they separated -- three different vehicles, three different directions.

Word had spread. They had come to see for themselves. Now they knew.

He turned to go back inside and nearly collided with the man standing just behind him outside the entrance.

***

The man was tall. Thin. His face was mapped with lines that suggested considerable age, though his hair was still dark. He wore a long coat that had seen better decades and carried a walking stick.

He was also, quite clearly, blind. His eyes were open but unfocused, staring at a point somewhere past Gregory's left shoulder.

"Forgive me," the man said. His accent was French. "I did not mean to startle you. I wanted to ensure the others had gone before I approached."

Gregory stepped to the side, making sure his footsteps were audible. "Please, come in."

They moved towards the entrance. Lawrence ducked as they passed through the low medieval doorway.

Inside, Gregory turned to face him properly. "I'm Father Gregory Chadwick."

The man smiled. It was a good smile, though it carried considerable sadness. "I know who you are. My name is Lawrence. I am one hundred and fifty-nine years old, and I have travelled from Marseille to see your church."

He said it without hesitation, without embarrassment. A statement of fact.

"I wanted to see for myself what they were talking about," Lawrence continued. "Hear your words. See your face. Verify that you are what they claim."

Gregory noted the irony of the words this blind man had chosen but said nothing. He gestured towards the interior of the church. "Would you like to sit?"

"Very much," Lawrence said.

Lawrence navigated the space with the particular confidence of someone who had spent a very long time learning to move through the world without sight. He did not stumble. Did not hesitate.

They settled into the front pew. Lawrence set the walking stick aside. "I can be real around you," he said quietly. "No need for the prop."

Margaret appeared with a tea tray.

"After-sermon tea," she announced, as though this were the most ordinary thing in the world. Which, Gregory supposed, it had become.

Lawrence turned his head towards her voice and inhaled deeply. "Oh, that's lovely. With honey. May I join you?"

"Of course," Margaret said. She poured without asking what he took. She no longer had to ask. She simply poured -- two cups, honey in both, the particular proportions that made the blood tea work. And a normal cup of tea for herself.

Lawrence accepted the cup and sipped. "Perfect," he said quietly.

They sat in comfortable silence for a moment. Outside, the marsh was conducting its usual afternoon business -- sheep complaining, watercourses running, the wind making its opinions known about the state of the reeds.

Lawrence set his cup down on a small shelf beside the pew. He did this without looking, without fumbling. He simply knew it was there.

Then he stood, turned in a slow circle, and made a clicking noise with his tongue.

Click. Pause. Click. Pause.

Margaret watched with undisguised fascination as Lawrence turned towards the north wall.

"Mice," he said, smiling. "They're enjoying the Liturgy of the Hours. Psalms 58, 83, and 109, if I'm not mistaken."

Gregory grinned despite himself. "They have excellent taste."

Lawrence made another clicking sound and turned towards the organ. He walked to it, running his hand lightly over the wood. "You have a grand organ. Built by Renatus Harris?" He leaned closer, inhaling. "He always favoured a certain type of wood. This is his work, I'm certain of it."

"I play," Margaret said.

Lawrence turned towards her voice. "Would you? Please. One of my few pleasures left to me is music."

Margaret looked at Gregory. He nodded.

She settled at the organ and began to play. The Blue Danube. The notes filled the church, bright and clear, the waltz lifting into the rafters and settling into the corners where the mice were presumably enjoying their psalms.

Lawrence stood very still. His expression shifted -- not quite tears, but something close. A profound stillness that suggested he was somewhere else entirely.

When Margaret finished, she returned to her seat. Poured more tea. Said nothing.

Lawrence sat down slowly, as though the music had taken something from him.

"I was born on the day he performed it for the first time," Lawrence said quietly. "The fifteenth of February 1867. Vienna. My mother told me the city was full of music that night. I've never heard it in a church till now."

He paused.

"It always had a heart. The church acoustics gave it a soul."

Margaret paused, teacup halfway to her mouth.

"How long have you been blind?" she asked gently.

Lawrence smiled. It was not a happy smile. "I was born blind. I actually hoped after I was..." He paused. "Well. There are certain things that never change."

He slumped slightly, the disappointment settling over him like a coat he had worn for a very long time.

The silence that followed was considerable.

Gregory sat with it. Did not try to fill it. Margaret poured more tea and said nothing. This was not a silence that required fixing. It simply required a witness.

Finally, Lawrence spoke again.

"I heard rumours," he said. "In France. Then in Belgium. Then in London. About a church. A priest. One of us. They said..." He stopped. Started again. "They said you offer a peaceful end."

Gregory nodded, then remembered Lawrence could not see the gesture. "Yes."

"I have lived one hundred and fifty-nine years," Lawrence said. "And in all that time, I knew of only two ways to stop. Someone drives a wooden stake through your heart. Or you commit an atrocity terrible enough that hunters find you and do the work themselves." He paused. "I did not have the stomach for the second. And the first required finding someone willing to kill me."

He turned his head towards Gregory, his unfocused eyes searching for something they could not see.

"I travelled from France to see for myself if what they said was true. To verify that someone like me might choose peace instead of violence. To know that when I am ready -- if I am ever ready -- there is a door that opens gently rather than one that must be broken down."

Gregory met his gaze, though Lawrence could not see him do it. "The door exists. It will remain open. You may come through it whenever you choose. No rush. No pressure. It will be here."

Lawrence exhaled slowly. A great weight shifting, though not leaving entirely.

"Thank you," he said. "I never expected tea and hospitality. I came only to verify. To see."

He paused, running his hand along the smooth wood of the pew.

"The journey from Marseille was long. I should find somewhere to rest."

Margaret stood. "You can stay here, if you like. We have warm spots in the garden. Phil favours the right-hand corner where the morning sun warms the earth. The rest are available."

Lawrence blinked. "Phil?"

"Attending a bitcoin seminar in London," Margaret said matter-of-factly. "He'll be back Tuesday."

She led Lawrence towards the back of the church, still speaking in that same practical tone. "If you're hungry, there's fresh cow blood in the white fridge in the kitchen. Warmer next to it. Please wash your cup when you're done."

Gregory watched them go -- Margaret explaining the garden layout, Lawrence listening with the careful attention of someone learning the geography of a place that might, someday, become important.

The garden behind St Thomas à Becket was not large, but it was well-tended. Margaret had been working on it for years -- first out of general churchwarden principle, and more recently with specific intent.

She showed Lawrence the spots where the earth was warmest. Described the location of each relative to the church walls, the angle of the sun, and the shelter from the wind. She did this without sentiment, without drama. Simply: here is where you might rest. Here is where Phil prefers. Here is where the roses grow.

Lawrence stood in the centre of the garden, turning slowly, clicking softly, building a map in his mind.

"I think I should like to stay a few days," Lawrence said. "If that's acceptable."

"Of course," Margaret said. "There's an excavation happening -- Roman ruins under the church. Tourists come and go constantly. No one will think anything of another visitor interested in history."

She showed him to the right-hand corner, the spot where Phil usually rested. "Earth here," she said. "Soft. Warm in the mornings."

Lawrence knelt, pressing his hands into the soil. "Perfect."

Margaret left him there and returned to the church. Gregory was still sitting in the front pew, his tea gone cold.

"He'll stay awhile," Margaret said.

"Good."

She sat down and picked up her own tea. "He's travelled a long way just to know the door exists."

"That's what we offer," Gregory said quietly. "Not pressure. Not expectation. Just the knowledge that when -- if -- someone is ready, there's a gentle way forward."

Margaret nodded. She stood, collected the tea things, and headed towards the kitchen.

Gregory sat in the quiet church and thought about blind men who had travelled across Europe just to verify that hope existed, and doors that opened gently for those who had spent lifetimes believing they must be broken down.

Outside, the marsh carried on with its usual business.

A man from France rested in warm earth and was grateful to know that when the time came -- if the time came -- he would not have to choose between violence and despair.

Not yet perhaps.

But the door would be there.

***

Chapter XVII — The Collaboration

"As iron sharpens iron, so one person sharpens another."
-- Proverbs 27:17

The text arrived on a Tuesday morning whilst Sarah was reviewing blood cultures.

"Are you free for lunch? I have some business in town and would like to explore a business idea with you. -- Umbra"

Four months had passed since Carey's death. Four months since she had watched him turn to dust in a mansion in Leeds, the thunderclap still ringing in her ears. Four months of returning to her normal routine -- plasma samples, research protocols, the quiet hum of centrifuges -- whilst carrying the weight of what she had witnessed.

She texted back: "Yes. When and where?"

The reply came immediately: "108 Brasserie. Harley Street. One o'clock?"

Sarah looked at her watch. It was half ten. She had time to finish the cultures, write up her notes, and walk downstairs.

***

108 Brasserie occupied the ground floor of the building where Sarah kept her office. She had walked past it countless times -- white tablecloths, polished silver, the sort of place where consultants took private patients for reassuringly expensive lunches. She had never actually eaten there.

Umbra was already seated when Sarah arrived. She wore a charcoal suit that probably cost more than Sarah's monthly salary and sat with the particular stillness that Sarah had come to associate with vampires. Not fidgeting. Not checking her phone. Simply waiting.

She was, Sarah noted, exceptionally well put together. Hair professionally styled, nails immaculate, the sort of polished presentation that suggested regular attention from people whose entire job was making other people look flawless.

She stood when Sarah approached. They shook hands.

"Thank you for meeting me," Umbra said. "I know this was short notice."

"It's fine," Sarah said. "I was curious."

They sat. A waiter appeared immediately -- the sort of immediate attention that suggested Umbra had been here before, or more likely, that she had the kind of presence that made staff appear without being summoned.

Umbra ordered a large salad. Sarah ordered shepherd's pie. The waiter asked about wine.

"The 1952 Château Lafite Rothschild Pauillac," Umbra said without consulting the wine list. She looked at Sarah. "Would you like some?"

Sarah declined.

"A glass, please," Umbra said to the waiter.

The waiter's expression did not change, though Sarah suspected the wine cost more than she made in a week. Possibly a month.

When the food arrived, Sarah watched with undisguised fascination as Umbra began eating her salad. Fork to mouth. Chewing. Swallowing. The movements were perfect -- natural, unhurried, the performance of someone who had done this so many times that it looked effortless.

Umbra looked up and grinned. "Must do this to conduct business."

Sarah smiled despite herself. "How long does it take? The purging, I mean."

"About twenty minutes. Thoroughly unpleasant. But necessary if one wants to operate in the daylight world without raising questions."

She took a sip of wine. Considered it. Her expression shifted -- genuine appreciation, the sort of focused attention a sommelier might give a rare vintage.

"Mature," she said quietly. "Savory. Cedar and tobacco. Dried cherry cola underneath. Tertiary notes -- truffle, graphite. Classic Pauillac in its twilight years."

Sarah watched her. "You actually enjoy it."

"Very much," Umbra said. "Enhanced senses, you see. I taste it more acutely than anyone else in this restaurant. Every note, every nuance. I get genuine pleasure from it." She paused. "I just can't digest it. My body rejects it entirely. But whilst it's in my mouth? It's extraordinary."

She took another sip. "I've had time to learn. A century gives you that luxury.

The terroir. What makes a '52 Lafite different from a '61. The craft behind it."

"The ultimate bulimic," Sarah said quietly.

Umbra laughed. It was a good laugh, genuine. "Precisely. I cultivate refined tastes for things my body fundamentally can't use."

"Umbra darling!"

They both looked up. Two women approached the table -- one tall and elegant in a flowing silk dress, the other shorter with cropped hair and a leather jacket. The taller one leaned in for air kisses. Umbra stood, returned them with practiced ease.

"Shandra," Umbra said warmly. "And Akky. What brings you to this unruly part of town?"

Shandra smiled. "Akky needed a medical exam. We thought we'd find a café for tea afterward." She glanced at the table. "May we join you?"

Umbra gestured towards Sarah. "This is Dr. Sarah Okonkwo. She's a hematologist consulting with the Plasma Institute. We were just having lunch and updating each other."

Sarah shook hands with both women.

"We're just finishing up," Umbra said smoothly. "But please, dine here, this place is excellent, and on me. We'll get together soon."

Shandra smiled. "Of course, darling. But do come by this week -- I just got the Printemps/Été from Paris, and you absolutely must see it."

Umbra signalled the waiter, who appeared immediately. Arranged a table for Shandra and Akky across the café. Made it look effortless.

When they were seated and occupied with menus, Umbra turned back to Sarah. Her expression shifted -- from social warmth to focused professionalism in the space of a breath.

"I didn't ask you here to discuss my dining habits," she said. "I have a business proposition for you."

She reached into a Hermès Taurillon Clemence Double Sens 36 beside her chair and withdrew a folder. Set it on the table between them.

"This is the patent for Carey's bovine plasma formula. The one I and others live on. The one that allows vampires to function without hunting." She opened the folder, revealing dense technical documentation. "I inherited it when he passed. Along with the Foundation, the research facilities, and several billion pounds in assets."

Sarah said nothing. Simply listened.

"The formula works," Umbra continued. "I know it works because I use it. But I don't understand the science. I have no idea how the blood sausage is made, as it were. And I need someone who does."

She reached into the bag again and produced a small cooler. Set it beside the folder.

"Six containers. Enough for you to analyse, reverse engineer, and compare to human blood. I want you to extract the nutrients, identify what makes it work, and tell me why it sustains a vampire when human blood leaves them chronically malnourished."

Sarah opened the cooler. The containers were clinical, properly sealed, and labelled with dates and batch numbers. Professional work.

Anyone watching would see exactly what they expected: a haematologist receiving samples from a Foundation executive. Nothing unusual. Nothing worth noting.

"What's the objective?" Sarah asked.

"I want to sell it as a human iron supplement," Umbra said. "Hide the fact that it will sustain a normal diet in a vampire. Position it as a legitimate consumer health product whilst building the infrastructure to distribute it globally to the people who actually need it."

Sarah considered this. It was elegant. A public product that solved a private problem. Regulatory approval. Distribution networks. No questions asked.

"Why not use your own labs?" Sarah asked. "The Foundation has world-class facilities."

"They work on curing blood-borne infections for mankind," Umbra said. "You understand the reason for separation."

Sarah did. The Foundation's research focused on treating pathogens, developing therapies, and conducting trials for diseases that kill humans. If those same labs suddenly pivoted to perfecting bovine plasma nutrition, questions would be asked. Priorities would be questioned. The separation was necessary.

"What's the compensation?" Sarah asked.

Umbra took another sip of wine. "Two million pounds. Cash. Deposited in a bank on the Isle of Man."

Sarah went very still.

Two million pounds. More money than she would make in a decade. Perhaps two decades. Enough to never worry about a mortgage, never stress about funding, never compromise on equipment or research time.

She thought about it for exactly ten seconds.

"One million," Sarah said. "And you buy my office top-of-the-line equipment with the other."

Umbra's smile widened. It was a good smile. Genuine. The smile of someone who had just found exactly the person they were looking for.

"One million wholesale," she said.

Which meant, Sarah, calculated quickly, that she would end up with roughly three million pounds in total value. A million in cash and two million in equipment purchased at wholesale prices that would have cost her twice that on the open market.

She extended her hand across the table.

Umbra shook it.

No contracts. No lawyers. No paperwork trail. Just two women who understood each other, conducting business over shepherd's pie and a salad that would be purged in an hour.

"When do you need it?" Sarah asked.

"No rush," Umbra said. "Do it properly. I'd rather wait six months for good science than have rushed work that can't stand scrutiny."

Sarah nodded. She understood. This wasn't just about formulating a product. It was about building something defensible. Something that could withstand regulatory review, medical questioning, and the scrutiny of a world that didn't know vampires existed.

"I'll need test subjects from your community," Sarah said. "To test nutritional markers, track improvements, and verify the formula works as claimed."

"I can arrange that," Umbra said. "How many do you need?"

"Twenty. Varied ages, varied time since transitioning. I want to see how it performs across different physiologies."

"Done."

They finished their lunch. Umbra ate her salad with the practiced ease of someone who had been performing normalcy for over a century. Sarah ate her shepherd's pie and thought about research protocols, nutrient profiles, and the fact that she was about to become very wealthy whilst solving a problem most of the world didn't know existed.

When the bill came, Umbra paid without looking at it. "Make sure to add five hundred quid on my card for my guests," she told the waiter. Left a tip that was probably more than the meal cost.

They stood. Shook hands again.

"Thank you," Umbra said. "Carey spent his life trying to cure this condition. I'm building the infrastructure to live with it. You're helping me do both. That matters."

Sarah nodded. She thought about the Iron Shield cure sitting in her lab upstairs. The cure that could reverse vampirism completely or allow a peaceful death. The cure Gregory Chadwick refused to take because he believed he needed the condition to serve properly.

Cure or infrastructure. Death or life. Both were necessary. Both were merciful.

"I'll start this week," Sarah said.

Umbra smiled. "Excellent."

She left first. Sarah watched her go -- a woman in a charcoal suit walking out into Harley Street sunlight, wearing UV contact lenses and carrying the weight of building a world that didn't officially exist.

Sarah returned to her office. Sat at her desk. Opened the patent file. The work began.

***

Chapter XVIII — The Absolution

"The LORD turn his face toward you and give you peace."
-- Numbers 6:26

They were having tea in the garden on a Tuesday afternoon when Lawrence told her.

Margaret had brought out the tray as she always did -- blood tea with honey for Lawrence, plain tea for herself. The familiar ritual had developed over the past week. Lawrence sat in his usual spot near the roses, the warm earth beneath him. The rose bushes were bare except for the first small buds, green promises of spring. The air smelled of wet earth and things preparing to wake.

Lawrence turned his face towards where Margaret sat. "Tell me about your grandmother. What do you remember of her?"

Margaret was quiet for a moment. "She was a vampire," she said simply. "I'm absolutely sure she was. But she was always warm and kind. Always there with toys for me, and money for my family when they were struggling. When I graduated from university, she had set up a fund for me -- enough to get a flat and have my adventure."

Lawrence smiled. "She sounds wonderful."

"She was."

They sat in silence for a moment. The marsh carried on with its usual business -- sheep complaining, watercourses running, the wind making its opinions known.

Lawrence set down his cup carefully. "I think I'm ready."

Margaret went still.

"When?" she asked simply.

"Soon," Lawrence said. "Here. By the roses. If that's acceptable."

"Of course it is."

They sat in silence for a moment.

Lawrence turned his head towards the rose bushes. "I've lived one hundred and fifty-nine years," he said quietly. "And in all that time, people looked at me with pity or fear. The poor blind man. The dangerous vampire. Never just... Lawrence."

He paused.

"Here, no one pities me. No one fears me. Strangers treat me kindly. You bring me tea. Phil complains good-naturedly about me stealing his sleeping spot." His voice went high in mock falsetto. "'And someone has been sleeping in my bed!'"

They both laughed.

Lawrence's voice returned to normal. "Gregory listens when I speak. I'm just accepted." He smiled. It was a peaceful smile. "That gave me permission to stop."

Margaret nodded. She understood completely.

"I will alert the vicar," she said. "He'll need to make arrangements."

"Thank you," Lawrence said. "For everything. The tea. The roses. The kindness."

Margaret stood and collected the tea things. "You're welcome."

She left him there, sitting peacefully in the garden, his face turned towards the late afternoon sun.

Gregory was in the vestry when Margaret found him. He was working on Sunday's sermon, surrounded by books and notes, the familiar chaos of preparation.

"Lawrence is ready," she said without preamble.

Gregory looked up. Set down his pen.

"When?"

"Soon. He wants it to be by the roses."

Gregory nodded slowly. He had known this might come. Had hoped, perhaps, that Lawrence would choose to stay. But this was not his decision to make.

"I'll need to contact Dr. Okonkwo," he said. "Arrange for the cure."

"Your appointment is Thursday," Margaret said. "Could you collect it then?"

Gregory considered this. His weekly blood work in London. Sarah was monitoring his condition, checking his levels, ensuring the chelated magnesium and bovine blood supplements were keeping him stable. He could ask her then.

"Yes," he said. "Brilliant idea. I'll speak with her on Thursday."

Margaret nodded and turned to leave.

"Margaret," Gregory said. She stopped. "How is he?"

"Peaceful," she said. "More peaceful than I've seen anyone in a very long time."

***

Thursday morning came grey and damp. Gregory took the train to London, watched the Kent countryside give way to suburbs, then the tightly packed streets of the city. He walked from the station to Sarah's office on Harley Street, the familiar route he had travelled every Thursday for over a year now.

Sarah was waiting when he arrived. She drew blood, checked his vitals, and asked the usual questions about appetite, energy levels, and any unusual symptoms. Everything was stable. The regime was working.

"There's something else," Gregory said as she labelled the vials.

Sarah looked up.

"A visitor at the church. Lawrence. He's one hundred and fifty-nine years old. He came to verify that the peaceful option existed." Gregory paused. "He's decided he's ready."

Sarah set down the vials carefully. "When?"

"This week. He wants it to be at the church. By the roses in the garden."

Sarah was quiet for a moment. Then she stood, walked to a small refrigerator in the corner of her office, and withdrew a sealed medical case. She set it on the desk between them.

"The Iron Shield cure," she said. "One dose. Keep it refrigerated until you're ready to use it. The injection is intramuscular -- upper arm, deltoid muscle. It works quickly. Within minutes."

She opened the case. Inside was a single syringe, pre-filled, sealed in sterile packaging.

"You've seen me administer it," Sarah said quietly. "With Carey. It's the same process."

Gregory looked at the syringe. Such a small thing. Such enormous weight.

"Thank you," he said.

Sarah closed the case and handed it to him. "Tell Lawrence... tell him it will be peaceful. No pain. Just warmth, and breathing, and then rest."

Gregory nodded. He stood, tucked the case carefully into his bag.

As he reached the door, Sarah spoke again.

"Gregory."

He turned.

"This is mercy," she said. "What you're offering. Remember that."

***

Friday arrived cool and clear. The marsh smelled of spring approaching -- wet earth, growing grass, the particular sharpness of things preparing for summer.

Gregory stood in the garden and watched the light begin to change. Twilight was coming. Lawrence had asked for twilight.

Margaret appeared with blankets. Spread them on the ground near the roses. Made the earth soft.

Ted arrived quietly and stood to the side. Said nothing. Simply present.

Phil came last, walking up the path from the village. He saw them gathered and stopped. In seventeen hundred years, he had never witnessed a peaceful death for one of his kind. He moved quietly to stand with the others.

Others stood at the edges of the garden. Five or six of them -- silent, respectful. A man with two children. An older woman, her hands shaking. A man in an expensive business suit with a personal assistant. They had come to bear witness.

Gregory saw them all standing very still at the edges of the garden. He heard no heartbeats. Even the children. Especially the children. He felt a moment of profound sadness -- vampire children who could never play, never be carefree, never simply be children. Just small figures frozen in eternal silence.

Everyone stood in the garden as the light turned gold. Gregory, Margaret, Ted, Phil. The witnesses at the edges. And Lawrence, seated on the blankets near the roses, his hands resting peacefully in his lap.

Gregory stepped forward. Cleared his throat. He did not have notes. Did not need them.

"I only met Lawrence a week ago," he said. "And in that week, this blind man has shown me more about what he has seen than a sighted man sees in a lifetime. He has taught me to see with my other faculties -- touch, sound, smell. My eyes are just one of many ways to see the world. And I am better for it."

He paused.

"Amazing grace, how sweet the sound, that saved a wretch like me. I once was lost, but now am found. Was blind, but now I see."

Margaret knelt beside Lawrence. She opened an alcohol swab and rubbed it gently on his upper arm.

Lawrence turned his head towards her. "Really?"

"It's what they did in the video," Margaret said.

Lawrence laughed. A good laugh, genuine and unexpected. "My end administered with the help of YouTube."

Margaret smiled despite herself. She withdrew the syringe from its sterile packaging. Her hands were steady.

"Thank you," Lawrence said quietly. "All of you. For letting me be just Lawrence."

Margaret injected him quickly, professionally. Withdrew the needle. Set it aside.

Lawrence lay back onto the blankets and crossed his arms over his chest. His face was peaceful. He turned it towards the sky, towards a sun he had never seen but could feel warming his skin.

He began to sing. His voice was deep, rich, carrying across the garden.

"Amazing grace, how sweet the sound..."

His voice grew softer.

"...that saved a wretch like me..."

Quieter still.

"...I once was lost, but now am found..."

A whisper.

"...was blind, but now I see..."

He drew breath for the next verse.

"Through many dangers, toils, and snares..."

His voice is barely audible now.

"...I have already come..."

One more breath.

"...'tis grace hath brought me safe thus far..."

His lips moved.

"...and grace will lead me... ho--"

His body turned to dust.

There was absolute silence.

Then the thunderclap.

It rolled across the marsh like the voice of God Himself, shaking the earth, rattling the church windows, sending the sheep scattering in panic. A single, clean sound from nowhere, announcing that Lawrence of Marseille had gone home.

Everyone stood in the garden as the echo faded. The dust settled gently onto the blankets, onto the roses, onto the warm earth where Lawrence had found peace.

No one spoke.

There was nothing to say.

After a long while, Margaret knelt and began to fold the blankets carefully, gathering the dust with gentle hands.

"We have tea and biscuits inside for anyone who is interested," she announced as the group prepared to depart.

***

Chapter XIX — The Windfall

"The kingdom of heaven is like treasure hidden in a field. When a man found it, he hid it again, and then in his joy went and sold all he had and bought that field." -- Matthew 13:44

Ted counted the Sunday collection the way he always did -- methodically, in the church office, with the door closed and his notebook open beside him.

Loose change first. Copper and silver were sorted into neat piles. Then the notes, smoothed flat and stacked by denomination. Then the envelopes from the standing order donors were opened carefully and recorded in the ledger.

It was quiet work. Meditative, almost. The sort of task that required attention but left the mind free to wander. Ted had been doing this for fifteen years. He knew the rhythm of it. Knew what a normal Sunday looked like -- twenty pounds in coins, perhaps forty in notes, another hundred from the standing orders.

This Sunday looked normal. Right up until it didn't.

Five coins at the bottom of the collection box. Heavier than they should be. Wrong colour. Wrong size. Ted picked one up, turned it over in his hand.

Gold.

Not gold-coloured. Not brass pretending to be valuable. Actual gold. He could feel the weight of it. See the detail in the engraving. An eagle on one side, a woman's profile on the other. Text he couldn't quite read in the dim office light.

He set it down carefully. Picked up another. Different design -- a man in profile, text in what looked like French. A third coin showed a crowned portrait, British lettering around the edge. The fourth had Cyrillic text and an imperial eagle.

The fifth coin was smaller. Different tone of gold. Covered in script Ted had never seen before.

Ted sat very still for a moment.

Then he did what any sensible person would do. He took out his phone, turned on the desk lamp, and photographed each coin. Front and back. Clear, focused images.

He opened Google on the computer. Selected the first photo. Clicked "Search by image."

The results loaded.

"1896 US Twenty Dollar Gold Piece - Liberty Head Double Eagle."

Ted clicked the link. Read the description. Looked at the estimated value. Set his jaw and moved to the next coin.

He photographed the second coin. Searched again.

"1803 French 40 Franc Gold Coin - Napoleon Bonaparte Consular Period."

The third coin.

"1887 British Gold Sovereign - Queen Victoria Jubilee Head."

The fourth coin.

"1855 Russian Imperial 5 Rouble - Alexander II."

Ted sat back in his chair. Four coins identified. Four small fortunes sitting in the collection box. He did some quick mental arithmetic based on the auction prices he was seeing online.

Then he photographed the fifth coin. The small one with the unfamiliar script.

He searched.

Google returned jewelry websites, modern replicas, nothing remotely close to what he was holding. He tried cropping the image, adjusting the lighting, searching different angles.

Nothing.

Whatever it was, Google had no idea. But Ted knew gold when he held it. And this was gold. Old gold. Possibly very old gold.

He looked at the five coins laid out on the desk in front of him. Did the arithmetic again, this time including a significant unknown for the fifth coin.

Somewhere between ten and fifteen thousand pounds. Possibly more. Sitting in the Sunday collection box. Mixed in with the two-pound coins and crumpled fivers.

He uttered an oath he had not said in a church in twenty years.

Then he stood up, wrapped the coins carefully in his handkerchief, and went to find the vicar.

Gregory was in the garden with Margaret, having their usual post-service tea. The spring air was warm, the rose bushes showing new growth, small green buds promising colour in a few weeks. His sermon had been about spring -- the flowers appearing on the earth, the time of singing having come.

Margaret poured tea from her own pot. Blood tea with honey for Gregory, plain tea for herself. The ritual was comfortable now.

"Good sermon," Margaret said. "Mrs. Phillips said it made her hopeful."

"That was the intent," Gregory said.

Ted appeared at the garden gate. His expression was the sort of carefully neutral that meant something had gone very wrong.

"Father," he said. "You need to see this."

Gregory set down his cup. "What is it?"

Ted walked over, withdrew a small cloth from his pocket, and unwrapped five gold coins onto the garden table between them.

They gleamed in the morning sunlight. Heavy. Substantial. Unmistakably real.

"Collection," Ted said flatly. "Mixed in with the pound coins and fivers."

Gregory picked up the nearest coin. An American eagle, dated 1896. He set it down, picked up another. French, Napoleon in profile. A third -- British, Queen Victoria.

Margaret leaned forward, studied them without touching. "From Friday," she said quietly. It was not a question.

"Most likely," Gregory agreed.

Ted pointed to the fourth coin. "Russian Imperial, 1855. Worth about two thousand pounds, near as I can tell." He paused. "Then there's this one."

He separated the fifth coin from the others. It was smaller, a different tone of gold, covered in script neither Gregory nor Ted recognised.

"Can't find anything on it," Ted said. "Google came back with nothing useful. The writing is... I don't know what that is."

Gregory picked it up. Turned it in the light. His enhanced vision caught details the others couldn't see -- fine engraving, worn edges, text so small it would be invisible to normal eyes.

He read the inscription carefully. "Sanskrit," he said quietly. "Gupta Empire. Fourth century."

Ted went very still. Did some mental arithmetic. "Oh fuc..."

He caught himself. But the meaning hung in the air regardless.

They sat there for a moment. Three people looking at five impossible coins, trying to work out what to do with them.

Ted broke the silence. "We need someone who's an expert on this old stuff."

"Phil," Gregory said.

"Phil," Margaret said at exactly the same moment.

"Phil," Ted agreed.

Margaret stood. Walked across the garden to the far corner where the morning sun warmed the earth. Phil's spot. She stood over it, looking down at the bare ground.

"Wake up, governor," she said clearly. "We need you."

She tipped her teacup slightly. A thin stream of tea splashed onto the earth.

For a moment, nothing happened.

Then the ground shifted. Dirt fell away in small cascades. A hand emerged, then an arm, then Phil's head breaking the surface like someone climbing out of a pool.

He blinked in the morning light. Brushed dirt from his hair. Looked at Margaret with an expression somewhere between annoyed and resigned.

"I was winning," he said.

Margaret raised an eyebrow. "Winning what?"

"Ludus Latrunculorum. Cassius was about to flip the board. Sore loser." He shook more dirt from his shoulders. "It was a very good dream."

He looked at the teacup in her hand. "Really? Tea?"

"It seemed efficient," Margaret said.

Phil climbed out of the earth, shook himself like a dog, and walked over to the table. Looked at the coins. His expression changed.

He picked up the Gupta dinar. Turned it over. Read the inscription.

"Chandragupta II," he said. "Reign of. Very rare. Museum quality." He set it down carefully. "Where did you get this?"

"Sunday collection," Ted said.

Phil looked at him. Then at Gregory. Then back at the coins.

"Ah," he said. "Friday's witnesses."

"That would be my assumption," Gregory said.

Phil sat down in the empty chair, still covered in dirt. Picked up each coin in turn. Examined them with the practiced eye of someone who had seen currencies come and go across two millennia.

"The American piece," he said. "Perhaps two thousand pounds. The Napoleon -- fifteen hundred. The Victorian sovereign -- a thousand. The Russian Imperial -- two thousand." He picked up the Gupta dinar again. "This one. Museum quality, fourth century, excellent condition. Eighteen to twenty thousand pounds to the right collector."

He set them all back down. Did the arithmetic.

"Twenty-five thousand pounds," Phil said. "Give or take."

No one spoke for a moment.

"You have a problem," Phil said finally.

"Yes," Gregory said. "We've noticed."

Ted cleared his throat. "Can't deposit them. Can't explain them. Can't pretend they don't exist."

"No," Gregory agreed.

He picked up his phone. Photographed each coin carefully.

Then he opened his messages and typed.

"We have a situation. Need your advice."

He attached the photos. Sent them to Umbra.

They waited.

The reply came at three o'clock that afternoon. Gregory's phone buzzed on the vestry desk where he'd been working on next Sunday's sermon.

"I see you had some ancient tourists visit."

Gregory smiled despite himself. Typed back: "Five of them. Left gratitude we can't explain."

The reply was immediate.

"I will handle them. Cash or Parish Giving?"

Gregory stared at the message. Typed: "What's Parish Giving?"

"Online donation platform," Umbra replied. "One thousand pounds weekly looks like organic growth. Legitimate. Traceable. Explainable. Diocese sees healthy online engagement, not ancient gold."

Gregory smiled. Of course.

Before he could respond, Margaret appeared in the doorway.

"We need a new organ," she said.

Gregory looked up. "What?"

"A new organ. I've been saying this since 1982."

Gregory looked at his phone. Looked at Margaret. Typed his response.

"Parish Giving."

Umbra: "Done. Send them to Leeds Castle. I'll have them collected."

Gregory set down his phone. Looked at Margaret. "The organ fund just received a significant donation."

Margaret smiled. It was a small smile, but genuine.

That evening, Gregory sat with Ted and Phil in the garden. The coins were wrapped again, ready to be posted the following morning.

"The French one," Gregory said. "That was Lawrence. I'm certain of it."

"The franc," Phil agreed. "From Marseille. His final gift."

"The others?" Ted asked.

Phil shrugged. "The man with the children, perhaps. The woman with the shaking hands. The businessman. Others stayed for tea afterward. We'll never know."

"Anonymous gratitude," Gregory said quietly.

"The best kind," Phil said.

***

Tuesday morning, Gregory's phone rang whilst he was reviewing the lectionary for next Sunday. He glanced at the screen. Umbra.

He answered. "Hello."

"Good news first," Umbra said without preamble. "The coins are handled. Sold quietly to collectors, I trust. Twenty-six thousand pounds total."

"That's excellent," Gregory said.

"Parish Giving will receive one thousand pounds weekly for the next twenty-six weeks. Stays under the radar. Looks like organic growth in online donations."

"Thank you," Gregory said. "Margaret will be pleased about the organ."

"I'm sure she will," Umbra said. "But Gregory, we have a larger issue to deal with."

Gregory went very still. "What issue?"

"The Diocese has discovered Carey's endowment."

Gregory blinked. "Carey's what?"

"The ten million pound endowment he established for St Thomas à Becket. You didn't know?"

"What ten million pound endowment?!" Gregory's voice went up half an octave.

There was a pause on the other end. "Oh," Umbra said. "He didn't tell you."

"No," Gregory said. "He most certainly did not."

"Well," Umbra said carefully. "He established a trust. Ten million pounds. Restricted use -- can only be spent on parish ministry, pastoral care, and building maintenance. The Diocese can't touch it."

Gregory sat down heavily in his chair.

"The problem," Umbra continued, "is the language in the trust documents. Carey wrote quite beautifully about your ministry. How you gave freely. Never asked for anything in return. Terrible for business, wonderful for people."

She paused.

"Gregory. The Diocese knows. And they'll have questions."

Gregory closed his eyes. Thought about Friday twilight. About Lawrence singing Amazing Grace. About vampire witnesses standing at the edges of the garden, bearing witness to mercy.

"Questions," he repeated quietly.

"Many questions," Umbra agreed. "About what services you provided that warranted a ten million pound gift. About the nature of your ministry. About why a billionaire business magnate chose a small parish church on Romney Marsh."

Gregory was quiet for a long moment.

"I have lawyers available if you need them," Umbra said.

"Thank you," Gregory said. "I suspect I might."

He hung up. Sat at his desk. Looked out the window at the garden where the roses were beginning to bud.

Twenty-six thousand pounds for a new organ.

Ten million pounds, the Diocese wanted to understand.

And somewhere in a mansion in Leeds, an ancient vampire had left one final gift -- and one final problem.

***

Chapter XX — The Lord Giveth

"Someone in the crowd said to him, 'Teacher, tell my brother to divide the inheritance with me." But he said to him, "Man, who made me a judge or arbitrator over you?" And he said to them, "Take care, and be on your guard against all covetousness, for one's life does not consist in the abundance of his possessions." -- Luke 12:13-15

The text arrived on Wednesday morning whilst Gregory was preparing for the midweek service.

A number he didn't recognize. A message with no greeting.

"Keep your life free from love of money, and be content with what you have, for he has said, 'I will never leave you nor forsake you.' -- Hebrews 13:5"

Gregory stared at the screen. Read it again. Understood immediately.

The Diocese. They knew about the endowment. And they were opening with scripture.

He sat down at his desk. Thought for a moment. Then typed his response. Slowly. Carefully. The full text of Luke chapter twelve, verses thirteen through twenty-one. The parable of the Rich Fool. Every word.

He read it over once. Then pressed send.

The reply came thirty seconds later.

"We need to have a meeting. St Mary's. Tomorrow at two o'clock."

Gregory set down his phone. Looked out the window at the garden where spring was arriving in small green increments. Then he stood, walked to the vestry, and found Ted replacing a burnt-out lightbulb.

"Ted," he said. "I need you to come with me tomorrow. St Mary's. The Diocese wants a meeting."

Ted climbed down from the stepladder. Set down the lightbulb. "About the endowment."

It was not a question.

"Yes," Gregory said.

Ted nodded once. "Two o'clock?"

"Two o'clock."

"I'll drive," Ted said.

St Mary's Cathedral sat in the centre of town like a medieval rebuke to modernity. Grey stone, Gothic arches, centuries of accumulated authority pressed into every carved detail. The administrative offices occupied the north transept -- newer construction, but attempting to match the original stonework with varying degrees of success.

Ted parked the car. Turned off the engine. Sat for a moment.

"Right then," he said finally.

They walked through the cathedral grounds. Past the gift shop. Through the cloister. Up a modern staircase to the second floor, where the administrative offices hummed with the quiet efficiency of ecclesiastical bureaucracy.

A secretary looked up as they entered. Smiled professionally. "Father Chadwick?"

"Yes," Gregory said.

"The Archdeacon is expecting you. Conference room two."

She gestured down a corridor. Gregory thanked her. He and Ted walked past framed photographs of previous bishops, past notice boards announcing committee meetings and diocesan events, to a door marked "Conference Room 2."

Gregory knocked. A voice called, "Come in."

They entered.

The Archdeacon sat at the head of the table. Sixties, perhaps. Grey hair, clerical collar, the sort of professional warmth that could turn cold with remarkable speed. Two assistants flanked him -- younger clergy, both taking notes on laptops.

"Father Chadwick," the Archdeacon said, rising slightly. "Thank you for coming. And this is..."

"Ted," Gregory said. "My churchwarden."

"Of course. Please, sit."

They sat. The Archdeacon folded his hands on the table.

"I'll be direct," he said. "We've become aware of a substantial endowment left to St Thomas à Becket. Ten million pounds. From a Mr. Kushim Arit."

Gregory said nothing.

"This is, of course, wonderful news," the Archdeacon continued. "A significant gift. We are very pleased."

He paused. Smiled. "However, an endowment of this size raises certain questions. Questions of stewardship. Proper oversight. The Diocese has a responsibility to ensure that resources -- especially resources of this magnitude -- benefit the broader church community."

One of the assistants looked up from his laptop. "Other parishes are struggling. Roofs need repair. Heating systems are failing. The diocesan budget is stretched thin."

The Archdeacon nodded. "Precisely. We want to ensure this gift is used wisely. For the good of all. Not just one parish."

Ted shifted in his chair. Gregory felt the movement but said nothing.

"Of course," the Archdeacon went on, his tone warming, "we want to make sure St Thomas à Becket has everything it needs. Any reasonable requests will be given full consideration. Anything at all."

Ted spoke for the first time. "Like the organ?"

The Archdeacon's smile flickered. "I'm sorry?"

"The organ," Ted said. "Been asking for one since 1982. Margaret has. Good woman, Margaret. Patient."

The Archdeacon glanced at his assistants. One of them tapped something into his laptop. "A church organ. That would be... substantial. Quite expensive. We're not sure the endowment was intended for that sort of expenditure."

"Exactly," Ted said.

Silence fell across the room.

The Archdeacon's expression cooled by several degrees. "I'm not sure I understand your point."

"You said anything?" Ted said. "Then you said not that. So, it's not anything. It's what you approve. Which means you're deciding how the money gets spent."

The Archdeacon sat back slightly. "The Diocese has a fiduciary responsibility--"

"The Diocese doesn't have the money," Ted said. "St Thomas à Becket does. The trust is very clear on that."

The second assistant spoke up, his voice carefully reasonable. "We're not suggesting the Diocese takes control of the funds. Simply that there should be proper oversight. Transparency. Given the size of the gift and the... unusual circumstances surrounding it."

"Unusual how?" Gregory asked quietly.

The Archdeacon leaned forward. "A billionaire business magnate leaves ten million pounds to a small parish church on Romney Marsh. No prior connection to the area. No history of charitable giving to the Church of England. It raises questions, Father Chadwick. Questions about the nature of your relationship with Mr. Arit. Questions about what services you might have provided to warrant such a substantial gift."

He let that hang in the air for a moment.

"This is a delicate situation," the Archdeacon continued. "Suspicions from others. Concerns of impropriety. It may threaten your position. We wouldn't want that."

Gregory smiled. It was a small smile, but genuine. "I am but a servant of the church. I will do what you see fit. But I have no control over the money. That is the churchwarden's job."

The Archdeacon and his assistants turned their attention to Ted.

Ted looked back at them. His expression did not change.

"Not a fucking chance in hell," he said clearly.

One of the assistants made a small noise. The other stopped typing. The Archdeacon went very still.

"That's highly inappropriate," the Archdeacon said. His voice had gone cold. "I understand you're upset, but we are all servants of the church here. There's no need for profanity."

Ted said nothing.

The Archdeacon's jaw tightened. "Let me be clear. If there are questions about the propriety of this endowment, there will be an investigation. A full review. We will examine every aspect of St Thomas à Becket's finances. Every transaction. Every relationship. The Bishop will be involved. Auditors will be brought in." He paused. "Your ministry will be scrutinised, Father Chadwick. Publicly. These things have a way of damaging reputations. Ending careers."

Gregory said nothing. Simply waited.

The Archdeacon looked at Ted. "Is that really what you want? An investigation? Auditors going through your books? Questions asked throughout the diocese about what's happening at St Thomas à Becket?"

Ted met his gaze. "With our lawyers present? With legal representation from the Arit Foundation? Our own accountants? And we also have the right to examine your accounting -- where the money would go if we agreed to hand it over?"

The temperature in the room dropped.

The Archdeacon blinked. Opened his mouth. Closed it again.

One of the assistants had gone pale. The other was staring at his laptop screen with sudden, intense focus.

"We don't need to involve lawyers," the Archdeacon said carefully. "This is a church matter. We can resolve it amongst ourselves."

"Can we," Ted said. It was not a question.

The Archdeacon glanced at his assistants. Neither of them met his eyes.

"We're all men of God here," the Archdeacon said. His voice had lost its edge entirely. "Surely we can find a reasonable solution. A compromise that serves everyone's interests."

"Not with threats we can't," Ted said. "Good day."

He stood. Turned towards the door.

Gregory shrugged slightly, smiled at the Archdeacon in what he hoped was an apologetic manner, and followed Ted out of the room.

They walked back through the corridors. Past the notice boards. Down the stairs. Through the cloister. Neither of them spoke until they reached the car.

Ted started the engine. Pulled out of the car park. A satisfied smile played at the corners of his mouth.

Gregory couldn't help but grin. "Where did you learn that move, Theodore?"

Ted's smile widened. "Watching the telly."

They drove back to Romney Marsh in comfortable silence.

The Diocese would be back, Gregory knew. With different tactics. Different pressure. But for now -- for this moment -- the endowment remained exactly where Carey had intended it to be.

With the church that gave freely and never asked for anything in return.

***

Chapter XXI — The Darkness Before

"I will turn the darkness before them into light, the rough places into level ground." -- Isaiah 42:16

Gregory could not sleep.

He lay in bed, staring at the ceiling, listening to the familiar sounds of the vicarage settling around him. The old pipes. The wind against the windows. The sheep complaining quietly to each other in the field beyond the garden.

But underneath it all, his mind would not stop.

The Archdeacon's face. The assistants taking notes. Ted's voice, flat and unmovable. "Not a fucking chance in hell."

The Diocese would be back. With lawyers. With auditors. With questions about the gold coins in the collection box. About Carey. About what services Gregory had provided to warrant ten million pounds.

He turned over. Closed his eyes. Tried to pray.

The words would not come.

Instead, he saw the Archdeacon opening the collection box. Finding the coins. Five gold pieces gleaming in his hands. The questions. The investigations. The end of everything.

Gregory sat up. Rubbed his face. Looked at the clock. Half past midnight.

He lay back down. Closed his eyes again.

This time, sleep came.

The Archdeacon sat at the head of the table. His collar was loose. His tie askew.

Gregory tried to stand. Couldn't move. His hands gripped the table.

One of the assistants moved behind him. Placed hands on Gregory's shoulders. Held him down.

The second assistant smiled. Fangs where teeth should be.

The Archdeacon stood. Walked around the table. His eyes had gone black.

"Questions about propriety," the Archdeacon said. He was very close now. his breath foul. "Questions about what you provided."

Gregory couldn't move. Couldn't speak. His hands clutched something. Heavy. Cold.

The gold coins. All five of them. Gripped in his fists.

"Your ministry will be scrutinised," the Archdeacon said. He leaned forward. "Publicly."

Gregory tried to scream. Nothing came out.

The Archdeacon bent to his throat. Teeth. Sharp. Breaking skin.

Blood shot from Gregory's neck. Dark. Fast. Splashed across the Archdeacon's white collar. Spraying across the table.

The coins slipped from his weakening hands. Fell to the floor. Clattering. Rolling away.

The Archdeacon's voice, thick with blood, husky. "They're mine now."

Gregory screamed.

Gregory woke with a start. His heart pounding. His hands shaking.

He sat up. Breathed. Looked at the clock. Quarter past one.

Forty-five minutes of sleep. That was all.

He lay back down. Tried again.

***

The earth was cool. Dark. Quiet.

Gregory dug with his hands. The soil came away easily. Soft spring earth, still damp from recent rain.

This was better. Safer. The ground would hold him. Keep him. No dreams here. No Diocese. No questions.

Just earth and silence.

He dug deeper. Made the hole wide enough. Long enough. Climbed down into it.

Lay on his back. The walls pressed against him. Cool. Steady.

He reached up. Pulled dirt down over himself. His chest. His shoulders. His face. Covering himself. Burying himself.

The weight of it. The comfort. The darkness.

He closed his eyes.

Rest. Finally. Rest.

***

Phil heard the digging around half past two.

Soft scraping sounds. Rhythmic. Close. Someone working the earth, maybe ten feet from where he rested.

He waited. Listened. The sound continued.

Then it stopped.

Phil rose from the ground. Shook off the dirt. Walked toward where the sound had been.

A hole. Fresh. Maybe three feet deep, six feet long. And the earth had been disturbed. Moved. Piled.

Someone was under there. Someone human.

Phil dropped to his knees. Started digging. Fast. Pulling away handfuls of dirt.

A face appeared. Gregory. Eyes closed. Not moving. Dirt covering his mouth, his nose.

"Gregory!" Phil pulled away more earth. Cleared his face. His chest.

No response.

Phil grabbed Gregory by the shoulders. Hauled him up and out of the hole. Laid him on the grass. Brushed dirt from his face.

Gregory's eyes opened. Unfocused. Confused. He coughed. Spat dirt.

"What are you doing?" Phil demanded.

Gregory blinked. Looked around. At the walls of earth. At Phil's face above him. At his own hands, still covered in soil.

"I..." He stopped. "I don't know."

"You were trying to sleep in the ground," Phil said. "You're not full vampire yet. You need air. You would have suffocated."

Gregory stared at him.

"Come on," Phil said. He hauled Gregory to his feet.

Gregory stood in the garden, swaying slightly. Dirt on his nightclothes. Dirt in his hair. His hands shaking.

"Stay here," Phil said. "Don't move."

He walked quickly toward the vicarage. Knocked on Ted's door.

Ted appeared within minutes. Took one look at Gregory and understood immediately that this was beyond his capacity to fix.

He went inside. Made a phone call.

Ten minutes later, his phone rang. He answered. Listened. Nodded.

"Twenty minutes," he said to Phil. "She's coming."

***

The helicopter came from the east. Low and fast, navigation lights blinking against the night sky. It circled once over the church, then descended toward the field beyond the garden.

The sheep scattered. Bleating in panic. Running in all directions as the downdraft flattened the grass and the aircraft settled onto the ground.

The rotors began to slow. The door opened.

Umbra stepped out in Dior athleisure. Laptop bag over her shoulder. She walked across the field as if landing helicopters in Romney Marsh at three in the morning was simply part of her weekly schedule.

Ted met her at the garden gate.

"Were you sleeping?" he asked.

"I was watching a documentary on humans crossing the Bering land bridge," Umbra said. "Where is he?"

Ted pointed. Gregory sat on a bench near the roses. Phil stood beside him. Both of them were watching her approach.

Umbra walked over. Set down her bag. Knelt in front of Gregory. Looked at his face. His hands. The dirt was still clinging to his clothes.

"When did you last eat?" she asked.

Gregory blinked. "What?"

"Blood. Supplements. When did you last have them?"

Gregory tried to think. "Thursday morning. Before the meeting."

Umbra glanced at her watch. "It's Friday. Three in the morning. You haven't eaten in nineteen hours."

She looked at Ted. "Get me blood from the fridge. Cold is fine. We need to get something in him now."

Ted turned and ran toward the vicarage.

Umbra sat down beside Gregory. "This is why you're in a state. Transitional vampires need regular intake. Miss a meal, and your biology starts compensating. Miss two and it gets dangerous."

"I was trying to sleep in the ground," Gregory said quietly.

"I know," Umbra said. "Phil told me. Your vampire instincts took over. The ground seemed safe. Restful. But you're not a full vampire yet. You still need air. You would have died."

Gregory said nothing.

Ted returned with a glass. Cold blood from the refrigerator. Dark red, almost black in the moonlight.

Umbra took it. Handed it to Gregory. "Drink."

Gregory drank. Slowly at first, then faster. The shaking in his hands began to ease.

"All of it," Umbra said.

He finished the glass. Set it down.

"Better?" Umbra asked.

"Yes," Gregory said. His voice was steadier now.

"Good. Margaret, are you awake?"

Margaret appeared from the darkness near the vicarage. She had been watching from the doorway. "Yes."

"Make him proper blood tea. Warm. With honey and the usual supplements. We need to do this right."

Margaret nodded and disappeared inside.

Umbra turned back to Gregory. "Now. Tell me about St Mary's."

***

They sat in the garden whilst Margaret prepared the tea. Gregory recounted the meeting. The Archdeacon's threats. Ted's response. The way it had ended with both sides retreating to regroup.

Umbra listened without interrupting. When he finished, she nodded.

"They'll be back," she said. "Different tactics. More pressure. But there are limits to what they can actually do."

"They threatened investigations," Gregory said. "Auditors. Public scrutiny."

"They can do that," Umbra agreed. "It's uncomfortable. It's invasive. But it's not fatal. The trust is ironclad. Carey's lawyers made absolutely certain of that. The Diocese cannot touch the money. They cannot force you to hand it over. They cannot redirect it."

She paused.

"What they can do is make your life difficult. Questions about propriety. Pressure from the Bishop. Making you justify every decision. That's the game they're playing."

"So what do we do?" Gregory asked.

Margaret returned with the blood tea. Warm. She handed it to Gregory. He wrapped his hands around the cup. Drank slowly.

Umbra watched him until the cup was empty. Then she spoke.

"Have you considered becoming a Self-Supporting Ministry, an SSM?"

Gregory looked up. "SSM?"

"Exactly. Self-Supporting Ministry status. You fund yourselves. Pay your own salary. Cover your own expenses. The Diocese handles staffing and sacramental oversight, but they can't control how you spend your money."

Ted leaned forward. "They'd lose their leverage."

"Precisely," Umbra said. "Right now, they pay Gregory's salary. They control the purse strings. That gives them power. Take that away, and all they have left are strongly worded letters and vague threats about impropriety."

Gregory was quiet for a moment. "The endowment could fund it."

"Easily," Umbra said. "Ten million pounds, properly managed, could fund St Thomas à Becket indefinitely. Salary. Maintenance. Margaret's organ. Everything."

Ted leaned back. "They'd never agree to just let us go."

"No," Umbra agreed. "They won't. They'll want their pound of flesh. Some concession that lets them save face. Tell the Bishop they got something out of the negotiation."

"What sort of concession?" Gregory asked.

Umbra thought for a moment. "The Roman ruins. They're bringing in tourists already, aren't they? Tourist revenue from that section. Any archaeological finds of value. That becomes diocesan property."

Ted nodded slowly. "Historical significance. Looks good for them publicly. Meanwhile, we keep the endowment and everything else."

"Precisely," Umbra said. "They get ongoing revenue from the ruins. You get financial independence for ministry. Both sides walk away with something."

She looked at Gregory. "It's a real negotiation. Not warfare. You offer them SSM status with the Roman section as their territory. Everything else -- the endowment, parish income, ministry funds -- stays with you."

"Will they agree?" Gregory asked.

"Eventually," Umbra said. "After they realise the alternative is a very expensive legal battle they cannot win. The trust is airtight. I have an entire legal team ready to defend it. They know this. They're hoping you'll fold under pressure."

She pulled out her phone. Made a note. "I'll have my lawyers draft a formal proposal. SSM status. Clear boundaries on the Roman section. Financial separation. You'll have it by Monday."

She looked up. "When they come back, you'll have a strategy. A plan. And you'll walk into the next meeting prepared."

She looked at Ted. "Keep him fed. No more skipped meals. Stress makes the biology worse."

Ted nodded. "Understood."

Umbra turned back to Gregory. "And you. If this happens again -- if you feel your control slipping -- call me immediately. Don't wait. Don't try to manage it alone."

"I will," Gregory said.

Umbra picked up her bag. "I'm staying until dawn. Make sure you're stable."

She walked toward the vicarage. Margaret showed her inside.

Gregory sat on the bench. The blood tea warm in his stomach. His hands steady. The darkness beginning to lift as the first hints of grey appeared on the eastern horizon.

Phil sat down beside him. "You scared the hell out of me."

"I scared myself," Gregory admitted.

"Don't do it again."

"I won't."

They sat together in comfortable silence. Watching the dawn come. The rough places are beginning to level. The darkness is turning slowly into light.

****

Chapter XXII — The Power of Vows

"And we know that for those who love God all things work together for good, for those who are called according to his purpose." -- Romans 8:28

The second meeting happened three weeks later.

Same cathedral. Same conference room. Same Archdeacon at the head of the table.

Different energy entirely.

The Archdeacon stood when Gregory and Ted entered. Shook hands. Gestured to chairs.

"Father Chadwick. Ted. Thank you for coming."

His assistants were there again. Laptops open. But they were taking notes, not preparing attacks.

"We've reviewed the proposal from the Arit Foundation," the Archdeacon said. "The Self-Supporting Ministry status. The financial arrangements. The division of responsibilities."

He paused. Folded his hands on the table.

"It's very thorough."

Gregory said nothing. Ted sat perfectly still.

"We believe this arrangement could work," the Archdeacon continued. "The Self-Supporting Ministry status gives St Thomas à Becket the independence it needs. The Roman section provides the Diocese with something of genuine historical value. Something we can manage properly for the community."

One of the assistants spoke up. Younger than the Archdeacon, clerical collar crisp. "Tourism revenue from the Roman section would benefit the wider diocese. Archaeological finds could be displayed properly. It's good stewardship of historical resources."

The Archdeacon nodded. "Precisely. And it allows St Thomas à Becket to focus on ministry without diocesan oversight of the endowment. Both sides benefit."

Ted glanced at Gregory. Gregory gave the slightest nod.

"We agree," Gregory said quietly. "The proposal is acceptable."

The Archdeacon exhaled. The tension in the room dropped by half.

"Excellent," the Archdeacon said. "We'll have the legal documents prepared. Self-Supporting Ministry status will be formalised within the month. The Roman section will be transferred to diocesan management with appropriate signage and access arrangements."

He stood. Extended his hand.

"I'm glad we could reach an understanding," the Archdeacon said. "This serves everyone's interests."

Gregory shook his hand. So did Ted.

They walked out of the conference room. Down the corridor. Through the cloister. Back to the car park.

Ted started the engine. Pulled out onto the road.

"Well," he said finally. "That went better."

"Yes," Gregory said. "It did."

***

The changes came gradually over the following year.

First, the surveyors. Then the architects. Then the construction crews.

A separate entrance was carved into the Roman section beneath the church. Modern stairs descending into ancient stonework. Proper lighting installed. Climate control to protect the mosaics.

A small museum rose beside it. Glass and stone, designed to complement the medieval church without competing with it. Inside: display cases for any artefacts found during excavation. Informational panels about Roman Britain. A timeline of the site.

The Diocese hired Phil to write some of the informational content. He was happy to help and declined any payment.

Then the gift shop. Postcards. Books about the Marsh. Replica Roman coins in small velvet bags.

The car park was expanded. Coaches could fit now. Tour groups arrived with regularity.

The Diocese hired staff. A curator. Two docents. Someone to manage bookings and educational visits.

The revenue reports came quarterly. Steady. Respectable. Something the Diocese could point to as good stewardship of historical resources.

And they left the parish alone.

***

Six months after the agreement, the Diocese sent a young deacon.

His name was Christopher. Mid-twenties, earnest, fresh from theological college. The Archdeacon presented it as assistance for Father Chadwick's growing ministry. Within six months, Christopher was ordained as a full priest in a ceremony that the Bishop himself attended.

Optics were maintained. Appearances preserved.

Christopher was kind. Hardworking. He handled the Sunday services at St Thomas à Becket and Thursdays when Gregory couldn't, freeing Gregory to focus on the Friday evening services that had become so well attended.

He noticed things, of course. The unusual attendees. The generous donations. The way certain parishioners avoided daylight services.

But Christopher was also remarkably incurious about things that were not his business. He did his work. Said his prayers. Helped where help was needed.

And he never asked questions Gregory would have to refuse to answer.

The donations continued. Friday services drew larger crowds. More testimonies of gratitude. More ancient coins are appearing in the collection box.

Umbra's dealer worked directly with Ted now. A quiet professional who asked no questions and provided documentation that would satisfy any auditor. The coins were sold discreetly. The money cleaned, blessed, untraceable.

But it no longer pooled in one place.

Under Umbra's direction, the flow was restructured. Regular donations appeared at all fourteen Romney Marsh churches:

- St Eanswith at Brenzett received funds for roof repairs.
- St Augustine at Brookland got a new heating system.
- All Saints at Burmarsh replaced its cracked bell.
- SS Peter & Paul at Dymchurch restored its medieval porch.
- St Thomas à Becket at Fairfield finally got its organ. Margaret supervised the installation personally.
- St George at Greatstone received funds for the community centre.
- St Peter at Ivychurch repaired its bell tower.
- All Saints at Lydd -- the Cathedral of the Marsh -- restored its war-damaged chancel completely.
- St Peter & St Paul at Newchurch replaced its south aisle windows.
- St Nicholas at New Romney received funding for electrical upgrades.
- St Clement at Old Romney repaired its Norman tower.
- St Dunstan at Snargate restored its beacon turret.
- St Mary the Virgin at St Mary in the Marsh replaced its Victorian spire.
- All Saints at St Mary's Bay received funding for accessibility improvements.

What had been a struggling cluster of forgotten churches became something else entirely. Roofs no longer leaked. Heating systems worked through the winter. Bell towers stood straight. The buildings were preserved.

Sustained not by faith alone, but by a network no one was willing to name.

Gregory stood in the garden on a Friday evening in late spring. The roses were in full bloom. The air smelled of honeysuckle and cut grass.

Inside the church, voices were singing. A hymn he recognised but couldn't quite name. The sound carried through the open windows.

Margaret appeared at his side. Handed him a cup of blood tea. Warm. The ritual comfortable now.

"The new organ sounds lovely," she said.

"Yes," Gregory agreed. "It does."

Ted walked over from the vestry. Phil climbed out of the earth near the roses, shaking dirt from his shoulders.

"Service starts in ten minutes," Ted said.

Phil brushed more dirt from his coat. "Who's coming tonight?"

"About forty," Ted said. "Three from Paris. One from Prague. The rest are regulars."

Gregory finished his tea. Set down the cup. Straightened his collar.

The arrangement held.

The Diocese had its Roman section. Revenue. Visibility. Something to show for its stewardship.

The fourteen churches had preservation. Roofs that didn't leak. Heating that worked. Bells that rang.

And the parish was left alone.

Gregory walked toward the church. The voices inside grew louder. A congregation gathering. People seeking mercy, counsel, or simply a place where they could be seen as human rather than monstrous.

He stepped through the door into the candlelight.

The congregation settled into the pews. Gregory stood at the altar. Looked out at the faces filling the church. Some he recognised. Some were new.

"For I was hungry and you gave me something to eat," he began. "I was thirsty, and you gave me something to drink. I was a stranger, and you invited me in."

He paused.

"The stranger is often unwelcome simply for being strange. But here, all are welcome. This is neutral ground. Even enemies may dine together in peace. You may rest without worry. Come and go as you please."

He closed his prayer book.

"A few announcements. We have free passes to the Roman section available for anyone interested. Guest quarters are available for travellers -- please speak with Ted or Phil after service. Pastoral counselling is available in the evenings by appointment -- speak with Margaret to arrange a time."

Margaret appeared from the vestry. "I've three pots of red tea with honey for anyone who'd like some."

"Thank you, Margaret," Gregory said.

And all things worked together for good.

***

Chapter XXIII — The Sustenance

"Feed the hungry, and help those in trouble. Then your light will shine out from the darkness, and the darkness around you will be as bright as noon." -- Isaiah 58:10

Umbra arrived at Sarah's office on Harley Street at ten o'clock sharp.

Sarah's receptionist showed her through. The office was the same as it had been months ago when they first met downstairs at 108 Brasserie -- clinical, professional, the sort of space that prioritised function over aesthetics.

Sarah stood when Umbra entered. She looked different. Not her appearance -- same lab coat, same practical hair pulled back. But her energy. There was something in her posture, in the way she moved, that Umbra had not seen before.

Excitement.

"Thank you for coming," Sarah said. "I have something to show you."

She gestured toward the conference room. Small. Glass walls. A table that could seat six but usually sat empty.

Umbra followed her in.

The table was covered. White paper printouts. Charts. Graphs. Sample bottles of V-sustenance -- Batch 15 in clinical containers. A laptop open to a presentation. Everything was arranged with the precision of someone who had been preparing for this moment.

Sarah closed the door. Turned to face Umbra.

"I finished the analysis," she said. "And what I found changes everything."

Umbra sat down. Sarah opened the laptop and turned it to face her. The first slide was simple. Two columns of data. Human blood. Fortified bovine plasma.

"Human blood," Sarah began, "provides basic caloric sustenance. Enough to keep a vampire alive."

She tapped the left column.

"But look at the micronutrient profile."

Umbra leaned forward. The numbers meant little individually. The pattern did not. Trace amounts. Inconsistent. Lacking.

"Vampiric physiology requires specific vitamins and minerals in concentrations far higher than what human blood provides. Iron, yes. B vitamins. Certain amino acids."

Sarah clicked to the next slide.

"When these are deficient, the body signals hunger."

A graph appeared. Feeding frequency plotted against nutritional satisfaction.

"A vampire could feed on six, eight, or ten humans and still experience deficiency. The hunger never resolves. It can't."

Umbra said nothing.

"The body isn't asking for more blood," Sarah continued. "It's asking for something that isn't there."

She paused.

"The psychological effects follow. Obsessive focus on feeding. Reduced capacity for anything else. Irritability. Impulsivity."

Another pause. Shorter this time.

"It's not a moral failing," Sarah said. "It's not inherent monstrosity."

She met Umbra's eyes.

"They're starving."

"They've always been starving."

Umbra sat very still. Her hands were resting on the table. Watching Sarah's face.

Sarah clicked to the next slide. The right column now. Fortified bovine plasma. The numbers were different. Complete. Sufficient. Optimal.

"Carey's formula provides everything the vampiric system needs. Complete nutrition in proper concentrations. When the body receives adequate nutrition, the hunger response disappears. Not diminishes. Disappears."

She looked at Umbra directly.

"The behavioural changes are remarkable. Increased emotional stability. Reduced predatory urgency. Expanded capacity for restraint, planning, and social integration. Vampires stop being survival-driven entities and become functionally stable individuals."

Umbra was quiet for a long moment.

Then she spoke. Her voice careful. Measured.

"I've been on Carey's formula for twenty-five years."

Sarah waited.

"I knew it worked," Umbra continued. "I could function. Conduct business. Walk in daylight with contact lenses. Eat food socially even though my body rejects it. I thought... I thought the formula simply sustained me. Prevented the need to hunt."

She paused.

"But that urgency you described. That obsessive focus. The hunger that never stops." She looked at Sarah. "I haven't felt that in twenty-five years. I'd forgotten what it was like. Until you said it out loud just now."

Sarah leaned back slightly. Watching the realisation move across Umbra's face.

"Before Carey's formula," Umbra said quietly, "I was always hunting. Always calculating. Every human I passed was potential sustenance. I couldn't stop thinking about it. Couldn't focus on anything else for long. The hunger was... constant."

She picked up one of the sample bottles. Studied it.

"For twenty-five years, I've been calm. Focused. I built businesses. Managed investments. Learned about wine for the pleasure of tasting it, knowing I'd purge it later. I thought that was just... discipline. Time. Maturity."

She set the bottle down.

"It was the food."

"It was the food," Sarah confirmed.

They sat in silence for a moment. The weight of that understanding settled between them.

Sarah picked up her white paper. Set it in front of Umbra.

"I've optimised the formula. This batch -- Batch 15 -- provides complete nutrition in a more stable, longer-lasting form. One bottle equals the nutritional equivalent of six human feedings."

She smiled slightly.

"There's something else. We tested different preservatives to extend shelf life. Honey works best. It adds flavour, but more importantly, it extends freshness by an additional week."

She paused.

"Margaret's been doing it right all along. The blood tea at St Thomas à Becket. She's been adding honey instinctively. Turns out she was optimising the formula without knowing it."

Umbra looked at the white paper. The charts. The sample bottles. Then back at Sarah.

"I want to do a limited run," she said. "Private label. Send it to the church. Let the congregation try it. People who are still living with that hunger you described. People who don't know it can stop."

Sarah nodded. "That's smart. Real-world testing with people who have reason to trust both you and Gregory."

"How many bottles?" Umbra asked.

"Fifty should cover the Friday congregation with enough for people to try multiple bottles and provide meaningful feedback."

"Done," Umbra said. "I'll have them bottled and delivered within the week."

She stood. Extended her hand.

"This is extraordinary work, Sarah. Carey spent his life trying to cure vampirism. You've given us a way to live with it. Both are necessary. Both are mercy."

Sarah shook her hand.

After Umbra left, Sarah sat alone in the conference room. Looked at the white paper. The charts. The sample bottles.

She had solved it. Proven it. Created something that would change lives.

And Gregory Chadwick still refused the cure.

***

The crates arrived on Thursday afternoon by refrigerated truck.

Ted signed for them. Carried them into the vestry. Opened one to inspect the contents.

Fifty glass bottles. Dark red liquid. Professional labels: V-sustenance -- Batch 15. Arit Foundation logo. Ingredients listed in small print. Nutritional information.

He picked one up. Read the label carefully. Set it back down.

"Looks professional," he said to Gregory, who had appeared in the doorway.

Gregory picked up a bottle. Studied it.

"We'll introduce it on Friday," he said. "These need to be refrigerated. Can we make room?"

Ted nodded. "I'll clear space in the kitchen."

***

Friday evening service drew the usual crowd. Perhaps forty people. Some regulars. Some from Paris. One from Amsterdam. A few new faces.

The service proceeded as always. Readings. Hymns. The sermon.

When the final hymn ended, Gregory stood at the front of the church.

"Before we have tea," he said, "I have an announcement. We have been sent bottles of fortified bovine plasma -- what sustains me -- and a request from Ms. Umbra Shadows of the Arit Foundation for you to try it, as a supplement for your current dietary needs."

He held up one of the bottles. The dark glass caught the candlelight.

"It's been optimised for complete nutrition. No pressure to try it. If you'd like some, speak with Ted after service."

He paused.

"If you prefer, Margaret has prepared three pots of red tea with honey for anyone who'd like some."

He set the bottle down on the altar.

The congregation moved toward the tea table. Some approached Ted about the bottles. Others hung back, watching.

Phil was first. He walked to Ted, who handed him a bottle from the cooler they'd brought from the kitchen.

"If Gregory's drinking it," Phil said, "it's good enough for me."

He opened it. Drank. His expression shifted. Surprise. Then something else.

Relief.

Others came forward. Ted handed out bottles. People opened them. Drank. Reactions varied -- curiosity, caution, then gradually, recognition.

An older woman -- one of the regulars, Gregory thought her name was Elise -- set down her empty bottle. Looked at Gregory with an expression he couldn't quite read.

"Three hundred years," she said quietly. "Three hundred years, and this is the first time I'm not hungry."

She paused.

"What sorcery is this?"

Gregory smiled. "Not sorcery. Science. Arit Foundation's labs discovered that human blood lacks essential nutrients. Your body's been signalling a deficiency for three centuries. This formula provides complete nutrition. One bottle equals the nutritional value of six feedings."

He gestured to the bottle.

"It's a superfood. For us. I've been living on bovine plasma for years now. This formulation is even better. The hunger can stop. Completely."

The room was very quiet. Then someone laughed. A good laugh. Genuine. The sound of relief after centuries of burden. Others joined in. Not mockery. Not disbelief. Just the pure, unexpected joy of discovering something you'd stopped believing was possible.

Gregory stood at the front of the church. Watching. Bearing witness to the moment when everything changed.

Not a cure. But something just as necessary.

A way to live.

Sunday morning service was busier than usual.

Christopher noticed immediately. Perhaps sixty people filled the pews, standing room only -- nearly double the typical Sunday attendance. He stood at the front, leading the service, and tried to place the faces. Some regulars. Many he didn't recognise.

Afterwards, in the vestry, he mentioned it to Gregory.

"The Roman section must be drawing visitors," Christopher said. "I saw several coaches in the car park."

Gregory nodded. "Possibly."

After Christopher left, Ted appeared in the doorway.

"All fifty bottles are gone," he said.

Gregory looked up. "Already?"

"Word spread quickly. People came back Saturday evening. This morning. Asking for more." Ted pulled out a small notebook. "I took notes on the feedback."

He flipped through the pages.

"One complaint. Copper taste. Several people mentioned it, but all said they didn't care."

Ted smiled slightly. "Extra bottles were requested. One young vampire laughed when I asked about refrigeration. 'I haven't had a refrigerator for fifteen years. No need for one.'"

He looked up. "The consistent hunger they've been feeling -- the hunger they've been ignoring for years, decades, centuries -- it's gone."

He read from his notes.

"Like a quiet that was so loud you could hear your heartbeat drumming in your ears." That's how one person described it. The absence of that constant hunger.

Gregory sat down heavily in the chair. Fifty bottles. Gone in less than three days.

"We need to tell Umbra," he said.

"Already did," Ted said. "She's scaling production."

Umbra had called Ted within hours of receiving his message. The feedback confirmed what Sarah's data had shown. This wasn't a Romney Marsh issue. This was global.

Production was the easy part. Distribution was the challenge. Vampires didn't have homes. Didn't have refrigerators. Couldn't receive deliveries. They needed to purchase it the way humans purchased anything -- from shops, gyms, and convenience stores. Places open at all hours.

But there was a deeper problem. There were no vampire gathering places. No community centres. No networks. The church at Romney Marsh was the first time vampires had ever congregated openly. The first safe space. The first community. Everywhere else, they were isolated. Hidden. Scattered.

She had the production facilities. Now she needed a way to reach people who had no addresses, no communities, no way to be found. It would take time. For now, locally. But the logistics were staggering.

She smiled slightly. Good problems. The kind she'd spent a century learning to solve.

Chapter XXIV — The Quiet Work

"Let all things be done decently and in order." -- 1 Corinthians 14:40

Over the next month was a whirlwind of activity.

With Gregory's permission, an outdoor pantry was installed beside the vestry wall. Brick to match the church. A simple door. No signage beyond a small placard: For those in need.

Inside, two commercial refrigerators. Stainless steel. Locked only at installation, then left open.

A separate power line was run from the road. It's own meter. The billing is sent directly to the Arit Foundation.

The Diocese was not involved.

No announcement was made.

The first delivery arrived before dawn.

A refrigerated lorry. Unmarked. It pulled into the car park, engine idling low. Two men unloaded crates into the pantry. No uniforms. No conversation beyond what was necessary.

Ted watched from the vestry window.

By the time he stepped outside, they were already gone.

He opened one of the refrigerators.

Glass bottles. Dark red. Labels clean and uniform.

V-sustenance -- Batch 16.

He closed the door.

It settled into rhythm quickly.

Every ten days, the lorry returned. Early morning. Quiet. Efficient.

The refrigerators were filled. Old bottles were removed, if there were any left.

No one waited for it.

They began to empty.

Not all at once. Not in any pattern Ted could easily follow.

One missing. Then three. Then a row.

By the fifth day, half gone.

By the tenth, almost nothing remained.

On the third cycle, Ted checked the pantry just before dusk. Three bottles left.

He stood there for a moment, hand resting on the door.

There was a small piece of paper tucked into the corner of the lower shelf. Folded once. Beside it sat a small gold bar.

Ted looked at it. Did not touch it.

He picked up the note. Opened it.

Thank you.

No name.

Ted looked at it for a moment, then folded it again and set it back under the bar where he found it.

He closed the refrigerator.

People came and went at all hours.

Some Gregory recognised from Friday services. Many he did not.

No one lingered.

No one took more than they needed.

No one spoke about it.

Quietly. Indirectly. Passed through Ted, through Margaret, through Umbra's channels.

The copper taste was mentioned.

Not as a complaint. As an observation.

Sarah adjusted the formulation.

Batch 17. Then 18.

The edge softened. Then disappeared.

No announcement was made.

The bottles simply improved.

By the end of the month, the pattern was clear.

The pantry was used.

The supply held.

No one abused it.

No one questioned it.

It existed.

And that was enough.

The first international call came three weeks after the pantry opened.

Umbra answered her mobile in the back of a taxi. London traffic. Late afternoon.

"This is Cormac," the voice said. Irish accent. Cork, maybe. "Someone who visited your church in Kent gave me a bottle. V-sustenance. Contact information was on the label."

Umbra waited.

"I've been hungry for two hundred and thirty years," Cormac continued. "I tried one bottle. That hunger stopped. Completely. I have a network in Dublin. Private. Quiet. How many bottles can you send me?"

"Five hundred," Umbra said. "Wholesale pricing. But they only stay good for two weeks. You'll need refrigeration and a reliable network to move them quickly."

"I have both," Cormac said. "And I can pay in gold bullion for a refrigerated van and cold storage unit. Build the infrastructure properly."

Umbra paused. Thought about it.

"Agreed," she said. "Send me your address. First shipment leaves Thursday."

She hung up.

The taxi crawled through traffic. Rain on the windows. London moving at its usual glacial pace.

Umbra sat back in her seat. Mind already working.

Cormac's request was simple enough. Five hundred bottles to Ireland. The Gloucester facility could handle that.

But if word spread to Dublin, it would spread to Paris. Then Berlin. Then Warsaw.

The Gloucester facility, near the Welsh border, could supply the UK and Ireland. Maybe France at a stretch.

But Central Europe? Eastern Europe? That needed local production. A second facility. Somewhere near a major meat processing plant. Lower transport costs. Faster distribution.

She pulled out her phone. Started drafting specifications before the first continental call even came.

Two weeks later, a call from Paris.

A contact in Dublin had told someone in France. The same story. The same request. Five hundred bottles. Gold for infrastructure.

Then Germany. Then Poland.

Each time, the same pattern. Someone had tried it. The hunger had stopped. They wanted to supply their network.

Each time, offers of gold. Centuries of accumulated wealth, finally useful for something beyond survival.

The call from Romania came on a Tuesday morning.

Umbra was in her office. Reviewing production schedules.

"We heard from Poland," the voice said. Accented English. Formal. "We have an established network. Carpathian region. Transylvania. Bucharest. We can distribute one thousand bottles. And we can fund an entire cold storage facility. Whatever infrastructure you need."

Umbra sat back in her chair.

Romania. The ancestral territory. One of the oldest networks. Of course, they were organised.

"One thousand bottles," she said. "First shipment in two weeks. I'll send you specifications for the Central European facility. We'll build it together."

She hung up. Opened the file she'd already created weeks ago. Updated the production estimates. - Ireland. France. Germany. Poland. Romania.

Five networks. Five distribution points. Vampire wealth building vampire infrastructure.

The production facility in Gloucester would need to scale. Quickly.

Good problems.

Umbra smiled.

***

Gregory stood in the garden one evening, watching the last of the light fade behind the hedgerow.

The pantry door opened. Closed.

Footsteps on gravel. Then silence.

He did not turn to look.

Margaret joined him, a cup of blood tea in her hands, for Gregory.

"It's working," she said.

"Yes," Gregory replied.

He watched the dark settle over the churchyard.

No announcements. No fanfare.

Just quiet work, done properly.

And people are no longer hungry.

***

Chapter XXV — The Celebration

"May he give you the desire of your heart and make all your plans succeed." -- Psalm 20:4

It was Margaret's sixty-fifth birthday.

The church was full long before the service began. Voices carried out into the garden. Coats piled where they could be hung. Someone had brought extra chairs. There were not enough.

There must have been three hundred people.

Some Gregory recognised. Many he did not.

Humans. Vampires. Travellers who had come and stayed. Others who had come only for this.

Margaret moved through them all, smiling, accepting embraces, shaking her head at the scale of it.

Gifts arrived from places she had never been. Small things. Thoughtful things. A few that were not small at all.

A parcel of tea from China -- Da Hong Pao, someone said, worth more than gold by the gram.

"You like tea," the man had said simply when he presented it to her.

Margaret shook her head at that, laughing softly, and set it aside with the others.

Then she saw Umbra.

She wasn't alone.

She had brought a guest.

"Nana?"

The woman smiled.

Margaret crossed the room in a moment. They held each other. Neither spoke for a long time.

Later, they sat together in the garden, away from the noise.

"How did you...?" Margaret asked.

"Your friend Umbra," her nana said. "She put out word she was looking for me. Wanted to talk. I was in Istanbul -- someone mentioned the V-drink she created. One thing led to another... and, well... here I am."

Margaret looked at her for a long moment, then took her hand.

"I thought I'd never see you again."

Her nana held her hand a moment longer.

"You could come with me," she said quietly. "We could travel. See everything together."

Margaret smiled. Shook her head.

"I've had a good run," she said. "Better than most."

She took her nana's hand.

"When it's my time, I'll go properly."

She paused, then added:

"And if St. Peter gives me any trouble, I'll kick him in the nutsack."

Nana laughed. So did Margaret.

They sat together and talked until the candles burned low.

***

Chapter XXVI — Methuselah

Though outwardly we are wasting away, yet inwardly we are being renewed day by day. -- 2 Corinthians 4:16

Ted was the first to notice.

Gregory seemed greyer. Not only his pale skin, but his hair had begun to show streaks of white. His face had softened slightly, the lines deeper than Ted remembered. Even his eyes seemed less bright.

They were lifting the ten-gallon container out of the back of Ted's Volvo when he mentioned it.

"You look tired," Ted said.

"I feel fine," Gregory said.

"Maybe you should start drinking that superfood Umbra provides," Ted suggested. "Extra nutrients you might be missing."

"I'll bring it up next time I'm in London," Gregory said, and brushed it aside.

But later, alone in the rectory, Gregory looked at himself in the mirror.

Ted was right. He did look tired. The white in his hair. The slight sag in his face. The eyes that seemed dimmer.

It had been ten years since Sir Edmund bit him. Ten years of ministry. Ten years of visitors and sermons and pastoral care. The stream of people needing help had grown larger. He welcomed all of them. Was happy to be of comfort to so many.

Maybe that was it. Maybe he was just tired from the work.

He was grateful for Father Christopher's help. The young man really cared about the people. It showed in his sermons, in his empathy.

Gregory turned from the mirror. Filed it away. Went back to his work.

His routine appointment with Sarah was the following Tuesday.

He had been seeing her weekly in the early years. Then fortnightly. Now monthly. Blood work. General examination. She had been monitoring his condition since the beginning.

He took the train to London. Arrived at her office mid-morning.

Sarah looked up when he entered. Her expression shifted slightly. Something he couldn't quite read.

"Gregory," she said. Standing. Coming around the desk. "You do look a little long in the tooth."

He smiled. "Teeth."

She smiled and then gestured to the examination chair.

"Sit. Let me take a look."

The usual blood draw. But then more. Skin samples from his arm. Nail clippings. A few strands of hair.

"Protein analysis," she explained. "Want to see what's happening at the cellular level."

Gregory watched her work. She was thorough. Methodical.

"How long will the results take?" he asked.

"A week. Maybe two." She labelled the samples. "I'll call you when I have something."

He left feeling vaguely unsettled. Not by the tests themselves. By the way she had looked at him.

Like she was seeing something he couldn't.

***

Sarah's call came three weeks later.

"I want you to come to London," she said. No preamble. "I've arranged some tests." "What kind of tests?"

"The thorough kind," she said. "MRI. PET scan. Full workup. I want to see what's happening inside."

"When can you come?"

Gregory looked at his calendar. Thursday service. Friday evening. Confirmation class on Saturday.

"Next week," he said.

Umbra's flat was in Kensington. Top floor. Tastefully furnished. Old paintings on the walls that probably belonged in museums. Above the fireplace hung a portrait of Carey.

"It's usually me and the cat," Umbra said. "Nice to have company. I'm well stocked with Red Cow -- that's what my creative department has named it."

She had insisted he stay there between appointments. The tests were spread across three days. Sarah wanted complete data.

The MRI was Monday morning. The PET scan Tuesday afternoon. Blood work. Tissue samples. A barrage of imaging that left Gregory feeling like a specimen.

Sarah said nothing during the tests. Just made notes. Reviewed scans. Her face gave nothing away.

Wednesday morning, she called him back to her office.

She had images up on her screen. Scans. Charts. Tissue analysis.

"Sit down, Gregory," she said quietly.

He sat.

She turned the screen towards him. Pointed to the images.

"This is cellular decay," she said. "Accelerated. Widespread. Your heart. Your liver. Your kidneys. All are showing significant deterioration."

Gregory looked at the scans. He didn't understand most of what he was seeing. But he understood her tone.

"How bad is it?" he asked.

Sarah was quiet for a moment. Then: "The mid-tier condition is burning you out. Your body is operating at a capacity that exceeds human limitations. Enhanced strength. Accelerated healing. Heightened senses. All of it requires energy. Resources. Your cells are working at 120% of normal human capacity."

She pulled up another image.

"The good news is your brain is protected. No decay there. Your mind is stable. Clear. That won't change."

"And the bad news?" Gregory asked.

"Everything else is deteriorating. Faster than normal ageing. If this continues..."

She stopped. Composed herself.

"You need the cure," she said. "Now."

Gregory looked at her. Then at the scans.

For a moment, he considered it. What it would mean to be human again. Just human. Ten years. Everything that had been done in that time. A breath of something like amusement passed through him.

"I have done my part."

He looked back at her.

"Then give it to me," he said.

***

The compatibility tests took two days.

Gregory stayed at Umbra's flat. Read. Prayed. Looked out at London and thought about everything that had happened in ten years.

Friday afternoon, Sarah called.

"I need you to come in," she said. "Both of you."

Her voice was different. Careful. Wrong.

They took a cab. Arrived within the hour.

She was waiting in her office. The door was closed.

Gregory sat down without being asked.

"Tell me," He said.

Sarah looked at Umbra. Umbra nodded once.

"The cure is incompatible," Sarah said. "Your body has adapted to the mid-tier state over ten years. The things that give you the extra abilities are fully bound to your organs. Taking the cure now would trigger catastrophic organ failure. You would die within forty-eight hours."

Silence.

Gregory sat very still. Processing.

"How long?" he asked.

Sarah's voice was steady. Professional. "At the rate of decay, you've physically aged twenty years in the ten that have transpired. Based on that, you have approximately five years left."

She paused.

"I would recommend switching to the fortified formula. The V-sustenance. Better nutrition might slow the progression." She looked at him. "You can still warm it, if that gives you comfort."

"Can you find another way?" he asked.

"I'm trying," she said. "I have equipment now. Resources. But Gregory..."

She stopped. Looked at him directly.

"I don't know if I can do it in time."

Gregory nodded once. Slowly.

Then he looked at Umbra.

"Did you know," he said. "When Carey studied me. When they developed the cure from my blood. Did you know the mid-tier was temporary? That it would burn me out?"

"We suspected," Umbra said quietly. "We didn't know for certain."

Gregory was quiet for a long moment.

Then he said, "The risk was worth it. I was the Rosetta Stone. The needed piece that made everything else work. My condition. My blood. The research you did on me—that's what developed the cure. That's what gave many a choice—a peaceful end, if they want it. A way back to humanity."

He looked at them both.

"I am one man who has helped many. Is there nothing less perfect than that?"

Neither Sarah nor Umbra spoke.

He stood.

"Thank you for the tests, Sarah. And for trying to find another way. But I think..." He paused. "I think this was my mission. This was my assignment. Seventeen years to build something that will last centuries."

He walked to the door. Stopped. Turned back.

"I am a man of God. If death is how I meet him, then it was the way God intended." A pause. "Seventeen years. Many helped. That's a life well lived."

And he left.

Umbra rose. "Well, there it is." And left as well.

Chapter XXVII — The Progression

Forget the former things; do not dwell on the past. See, I am doing a new thing! Now it springs up; do you not perceive it? I am making a way in the wilderness and streams in the wasteland.
-- Isaiah 43:18-19

Gregory returned to Romney Marsh on Saturday morning.

Ted collected him from the station. Said nothing about London. Didn't ask. Gregory was grateful for that.

They drove in silence. The marsh stretched out on both sides. Grey sky. Wind moving through the grass.

Gregory looked at his hands. Five years. That was what Sarah had said. Five years left.

He thought about what needed to be done. The confirmation class. Thursday services. The pantry restocking. Pastoral visits. Letters to answer. People who needed help.

Five years wasn't long enough. Not nearly.

So he would work faster.

***

Christopher noticed it first.

Gregory had always been thorough. Attentive. Present. But now there was something more. An intensity.

Thursday services ran longer. More visitors. Gregory spoke with each one. Gave them time. Never rushed.

Friday mornings, Gregory was already in the vestry when Christopher arrived. Letters written. Preparations made. Work done before the day properly began.

"Are you all right?" Christopher asked once.

"I'm well," Gregory said. "Just making the most of the time."

Christopher didn't press. But he watched.

The visitor arrived on a Friday evening in late October.

Service had ended. Most had left. A few remained, speaking quietly near the door.

Gregory saw him sitting alone in the back pew. Older. Weathered. Hands folded in his lap. He hadn't moved since the service ended.

Gregory finished speaking with Mrs. Alderton. Saw the last visitors out. Then walked back to where the man sat.

"Good evening," Gregory said.

The man looked up. His eyes were pale. Distant. But not unkind.

"Good evening, Father."

Gregory sat down in the pew beside him. The candles were burning low. Outside, the light was fading.

"Have you travelled far?" Gregory asked.

The man was quiet for a moment. Then: "I don't remember."

Gregory nodded. Waited.

Silence settled between them. The church creaked softly. Wind against the windows.

"My name is Gregory," he said gently. "What was your name?"

The man looked at his hands. Studied them. His fingers moved slightly, as though searching for something in the gesture.

"I am..." He stopped. Started again. "I am... I do not remember my name."

His eyes were sad. The kind of sadness that had settled in long ago and made a home.

Gregory let the silence sit. No rush. No pressure.

"What do you remember?" he asked.

The man was quiet for a long moment. Then, simply:

"Her name was Angelic."

He said it as fact. Not as an explanation. Just the truth of what remained.

Gregory understood. He had heard this before. Different words. Same weight.

"Where do you live?" Gregory asked.

"I don't." The man looked around the church. "I wake. I eat. I sleep. I wake again."

A pause.

"I only found this church when someone mentioned you had nourishment that didn't require violence."

Gregory nodded slowly. Understanding settling.

"Have you eaten today?" he asked.

The man shook his head.

"Would you like a meal? A warm place to sleep?" Gregory paused. "When you're rested enough, I can show you the grounds. If you'd like."

The man looked at him. Something shifted in his expression. A light that was not there before.

"Yes," he said quietly. "Thank you."

***

The next morning, the man was walking slowly along the path near the church. Looking. Taking it in.

Margaret saw him from the garden. Set down her tools and walked over.

"Good morning," she said. "Father Gregory said we had a new guest."

The man turned. Nodded.

"Are you hungry?" Margaret asked. "Would you like to see the church?"

"I would," he said.

She showed him inside first. The nave. The vestry. The small room where they kept supplies. Simple. Practical. No grand tour. Just what was there.

Then she led him outside. Around the building. Past the rectory.

They came to the garden.

The man stopped.

The roses were in late bloom. Reds and whites. Some yellows. The scent carried on the morning air.

He walked closer. Slowly. Leant in. Breathed.

Then he smiled. A sad smile. Small. But real.

"It reminds me of her," he said quietly.

Margaret watched him for a moment. Then, gently:

"Tell me about her. She sounds wonderful."

The man was quiet for a long moment. Then he sat down on the bench near the roses. Margaret sat beside him.

"I remember meeting her," he said. "She sold flowers. Gave me one because I looked sad."

A pause. His hands tightened slightly.

"I was a vampire. I hated killing. I tried..." His voice caught. "I tried drinking rats' blood. I tried everything. I tried..."

He broke.

The sob came from somewhere deep. Five hundred years deep. His face was streaked with blood tears.

Margaret didn't move. Just sat with him. Let it come.

After a while, he wiped his face. Breathed. Continued.

"She didn't pity me. She saw me as a person. Lost. She took me in. Gave me shelter."

He looked at Margaret.

"When I revealed I was a vampire, she wasn't afraid. She said... she said, 'Finally, someone strong.'"

Margaret nodded. Understanding.

"She brought pigs for me to drink from. Then she cooked and ate the meat. We talked. Forever, it seemed. She slept in my arms."

His voice softened. Remembering.

"I grew stronger. I worked. Earned money for the first time. Having it meant she could live better. We both worked. We cared about each other."

A pause. Longer this time.

"I have never been happier. She and I were together. We were together..."

He couldn't finish. The words caught.

"I don't know how long. It feels like it was just yesterday."

Margaret waited.

"She got sick," he said. "I had no ability to help her. The doctor didn't know what her ailment was."

His hands clenched.

"I talked with her about joining me. As a vampire. Before she could decide..." He stopped. "She was gone."

Silence settled over the garden. Just the wind. The roses moving slightly.

"I buried her by the roses. She always smelled of roses." A pause. "I don't see her face anymore. But I remember the roses."

Margaret sat with that. Let it breathe.

Then, gently: "What was her name?"

The man smiled. Small. Real.

"It was Angelic."

Margaret nodded. Stood. Brushed off her hands.

"I need help with my roses," she said. "We need to get them ready for the winter. Would you help me?"

The man looked up at her. Something changed in his expression.

For the first time in... he couldn't remember... he smiled. A real smile.

"I would love nothing more than helping you," he said. Then, quietly: "But I don't want to be a burden."

Margaret smiled. "We have a glorious supply of food. Plenty of space for you to sleep. There's a spot where the sun hits in the morning and warms the earth."

The man stood. Nodded.

Gregory walked up just then. "Ready for your tour?"

Margaret grinned. "Already did it. He's going to stay awhile if that's all right with you?"

Gregory smiled. "It's more than all right."

Margaret looked at the man. Considered.

"I'm going to call you Roy," she said. "You look like a Roy."

The man tilted his head. Considered it.

"I rather fancy that name," he said. "So be it. I am Roy."

Roy stayed the winter.

He worked in the garden. Then on the grass. Then the land around the church. He planted a vegetable garden. Worked beside Ted, getting the earth ready for spring planting.

He was amazed at how well he felt.

He wasn't hungry. Not just fed, but not haunted by hunger anymore. The constant gnawing that had followed him for centuries -- gone.

He slept better. The nightmares that had filled most of his sleeping hours -- five hundred years of faces, of violence, of guilt -- were gone.

He woke rested. Clear.

Spring came. Things were planted. The garden took shape.

One afternoon, Roy and Gregory sat together looking at the perfect rows of vegetables. The work done. Everything in place.

"Father," Roy said quietly.

Gregory waited.

"I have never been happier. But I am tired and want to sleep." He paused. "Margaret told me you can help me."

Gregory felt the weight of it. The choice being made.

"You can do so much more," Gregory said. "You can stay here as long as you like." Roy grinned. "I can, and I know I can. But I miss my Angelic, and I want to be with her."

He looked at the garden. The first green poking through the ground.

"I have more work to do," he said. "But with her. Together."

Gregory nodded slowly. Understanding.

"I do have a request, Father," Roy said. "Can I be buried with the roses? They're opening up. Welcoming me. I see her face in them, wanting me to join."

Gregory's throat tightened. After five hundred years of not seeing her face, Roy saw it now. In the roses. At the end.

"Yes," Gregory said. "Of course."

Sarah brought the cure three days later.

She arrived in the evening. Spoke with Gregory first. Then with Roy. Explained what would happen. How long it would take.

He listened. Nodded. Asked no questions.

The garden was quiet. Dusk settling. The roses just opening up, bees flying near them.

Margaret had set out a blanket near the bushes Roy had tended most carefully. The ones at the back. The oldest ones.

Roy walked out slowly. Knelt. Then lay down.

Sarah administered the cure. He closed his eyes.

For a moment, nothing. Then his breathing changed. Slowed. Deepened. Gregory stood nearby. Margaret sat on the bench. Sarah remained close, watching.

Roy's hand moved slightly. Touched the earth beside him. Fingers in the soil near the roots.

He breathed in once more. The scent of roses.

Softer than he remembered. But close enough.

He said, "I will see you soon, my Angelic." Then he was still.

It was done.

Gregory noted there was no thunderclap. Just a rush of wind.

They gathered the dust and added it to the soil in the garden. Near the roses he had tended.

No marker. No ceremony beyond a simple prayer, Gregory offered.

Margaret continued her work the next morning. Tending the same bushes. Watering. Trimming what needed trimming.

The garden carried on.

A week later, Ted mentioned the roses looked particularly strong this year.

Margaret said, "I think I am going to name this part 'the heirloom.'"

Gregory paused near the garden that evening. Looked at where Roy had worked. The roses blooming there.

Then he turned and went back inside. There was work to be done.

Chapter XXVIII — The Diminution of Life

He will wipe away every tear from their eyes, and death shall be no more, neither shall there be mourning, nor crying, nor pain anymore. - - Revelation 21:4

Phil found Margaret in the garden on a Tuesday afternoon.

She was deadheading roses. The autumn sun was warm. Everything quiet.

He walked over with his hands in his pockets. Grinning.

"Margaret," he said.

She looked up. "What have you done?"

His grin widened. He pulled two coins from his pocket. Held them out.

They were odd things. Half stone, half metal. Hybrid pieces from the Roman dig.

"Nicked them from the site," Phil said proudly. "The diocese is supposed to get everything, but these? These I am keeping."

Margaret tutted. But she was smiling. "You're impossible."

"I know," Phil said.

Then Margaret's smile froze.

Her face went pale. The pruning shears dropped from her hand. She collapsed.

Phil moved. Vampire fast. Caught her before she hit the ground. Lowered her gently to the grass.

"Margaret?" His voice cracked. "Margaret!"

She was breathing. Barely. Her eyes closed.

Phil looked around. Panic rising. He bolted for the rectory.

Gregory wasn't there.

He ran to Ted's workshop. Burst through the door.

"Ted!" Phil's voice was ragged. "Something's wrong with Margaret!"

Ted dropped his tools and ran.

They knelt beside her in the garden. Margaret's breathing was shallow. Laboured.

Ted pressed two fingers to her neck. Checking her pulse. His face went grey.

"Hospital's an hour and a half away," Ted said. "She won't make it."

Phil looked at him. "Call Umbra."

Ted pulled out his phone. Dialled. His hands shook.

Twenty-five minutes later, they heard it. The helicopter.

It landed in the field beside the church. Umbra stepped out carrying a portable oxygen tank. Moved fast.

She knelt. Fitted the mask over Margaret's face. Checked her vitals without speaking.

Then she looked at Phil and Ted. "Help me get her to the helicopter."

They lifted her carefully. Carried her across the grass.

As they secured her inside, Umbra pulled out her phone. Dialled.

"Gregory," she said when he answered. "It's Margaret. We're taking her to London. Meet us at The Royal London Hospital in Whitechapel."

The helicopter lifted. Phil and Ted stood watching until it disappeared. Gregory had been in town when his phone rang. He'd just finished pastoral visits.

Umbra's voice. The words. Margaret.

He got a cab. Sat in the back. Watched London pass. Prayed.

The Royal London Hospital in Whitechapel. He found Phil in the waiting area.

Phil, who was already pale, looked paler still. Almost translucent.

"Massive heart attack," Phil said quietly. "She's in the ICU. The doctors say she doesn't have long."

He stopped. Swallowed.

"She wants to see you."

Gregory nodded. Couldn't speak. Just nodded.

Phil pointed him towards the ICU.

Umbra stood outside Margaret's room. Arms crossed. Still as stone.

A nurse approached. "I'm sorry, but visiting hours--"

Umbra looked at her.

Just looked.

The nurse stepped back. Paled. Turned and walked away quickly.

Gregory arrived. Umbra glanced at him. Said nothing. Didn't need to.

She stepped aside.

Gregory pushed open the door.

Tubes everywhere. Monitors beeping. Margaret is in bed. Small. Fragile in a way she'd never been.

Her breathing was raspy. Laboured.

He moved to the side of the bed. Sat in the chair beside her.

Her eyes opened. Slowly. Found him.

"Father... Gregory..." Her voice barely there. "I'm sorry."

Gregory started sobbing. His face coated in blood tears.

Margaret tutted. "Wipe your face. You're an embarrassment."

He grabbed a napkin from the bedside table. Tried to wipe his face. Just ended up smearing it. His complexion bright pink now.

Margaret almost smiled. Almost.

"Bury me by the roses," she said. Each word an effort. "I want to be with my friends."

"I promise," Gregory managed.

Margaret's eyes stayed on his. "You'd better hurry with those prayers. I think God wants me now and is impatient."

Gregory nodded. Tried to steady his voice.

He began. "Thou shalt sprinkle me with hyssop, and I shall be..."

The monitor beside the bed began a steady tone.

Long. Unbroken.

She had died before he could finish.

Gregory's voice broke. But he continued. Crying through the words. Finishing the prayer over her still form.

The door opened. Ted rushed in. Then Umbra. Phil behind them.

They stood there. Silent. While Gregory finished the last rites through his tears.

When he was done, none of them moved.

Margaret was gone.

***

Hundreds came to the funeral.

People who had met her. Loved her. Been helped by her. They filled the church and stood outside.

Margaret's granddaughter was there with her husband and two children. All of them quiet. Grief-stricken.

A woman sat near them. Younger-looking. Introduced herself as Margaret's estranged sister who had been away for years.

Nana.

The Bishop officiated. Formal. Proper. Every word measured.

Ted read some of Margaret's poems. His voice was steady at first. Then breaking. By the third one, he couldn't finish. Just folded the paper and sat down.

His wife sat beside him. Sobbing quietly. Ted, normally so stoic, wiped at his eyes. Again, and again.

An organist from another marsh parish played Margaret's favoured pieces. Bach. Handel. The music filled the church.

Then Gregory stood for the eulogy.

He looked out at the crowd. At all the faces. Cleared his throat.

"At Margaret's birthday, she was gifted tea from China. After drinking it, she said it 'ruined English breakfast tea forever.'"

A few people smiled. Remembering.

"Margaret enjoyed life. She was loved by everyone she met. She did not speak much, but when she talked, you listened. Because she would usually be right."

He paused. Steadied himself.

"She requested her ashes be buried by the rose bushes. And that is what we are doing. A new bench has been donated as well and will be known hereafter as the heirloom."

His voice cracked.

"I will miss her dearly. And this place will never be the same without her here."

He sat down.

The service ended. People filed out slowly. No one rushed.

Umbra stood near the back with several vampires. Showing respect. Speaking in low tones. Organising them.

A network of distributors for V-Sustenance. It would be ready for the mass market within the year, pending government approvals.

Even here, she worked.

They buried her ashes in The Heirloom. Near the roses. Where Roy rested. Where Laurence had been laid years before.

The new bench sat nearby. Simple wood. Well-made. A small brass plate fixed to the back.

"The Heirloom."

Gregory stood there after everyone left. Looking at the roses. The bench. The ground where Margaret now rested.

The garden carried on.

It always would.

Chapter XXIX — The Quietude

But the Lord is in his holy temple; let all the earth keep silence before him. -- Habakkuk 2:20

There seemed to be a hush at St. Thomas à Becket.

People spoke softly. Even the sheep in the fields seemed respectfully quiet. A pallor of sadness had crept over the place.

It had been a year since Margaret passed, and it still felt like it had just happened.

A new assistant churchwarden had been hired. A large Irish woman with a bawdy sense of humour that Ted appreciated. She was efficient. Kind. But she wasn't Margaret.

Margaret's ghost haunted the place. Not literally. But in the way absence does.

The roses were especially lush and hardy this year. Their own private celebration. Everyone who walked past them swore they heard Margaret's voice.

"Mind your step. We are resting here."

Gregory often sat on the bench in The Heirloom. Having private conversations with her. Talking to the roses as though she might answer.

He seemed dimmer. Less active. As if the life force was leaking from his body.

Whether it was advancing age or sadness, no one could say. Perhaps both.

Father Christopher was doing the brunt of the services at this point. Morning mass. Evening prayers. Pastoral visits. Gregory attended, but more as a presence than a participant.

After morning mass one Tuesday, Gregory requested that Christopher join him.

Gregory was sitting on the bench when Christopher arrived. The bench in the garden. The brass plate reading "The Heirloom" catches the morning light.

Christopher sat beside him. Waited.

"Father," Gregory said. "I would like to talk to you about our congregation."

Christopher was a little surprised to be addressed so formally. But he nodded. "Go on."

Gregory looked at his hands. He had been preparing this talk for a long time. But at this moment, he found it harder to say out loud than he'd thought.

"I am sure you have noticed there are always new faces showing," Gregory said.

"Yes. The Roman fort gets many travellers who stay for the services."

Gregory smiled. "Yes. Them too." He took a deep breath. "But there are others."

Christopher nodded slowly. "The paler ones. They sit very still. They never fidget. They never need to read a Bible. It's as if they've memorised them."

Gregory nodded. "Yes. Them." He sat up a bit straighter. "They are vampires."

Christopher laughed suddenly. "A vampire in a church. That is a laugh."

Gregory said nothing. Just looked at him.

"I am serious," Gregory said.

Christopher looked at Gregory. Really looked at him. Waiting for the punchline that never came.

"How?" Christopher asked finally.

"Well, first..." Gregory paused. "I am also a vampire. Well, not fully. But mostly."

Christopher stared at him. "You are one of the most devoted, holiest men I have ever met. And you're a drinker of blood who..."

"The pantry," Gregory interrupted gently. "The one outside. Do you know what it contains?"

"A sustenance for the poor, I assume. Some kind of meal replacement."

Gregory smiled. "I suppose you're right on that one. I never thought about it that way. Have you ever drunk one?"

"No. They're for people who have little or nothing. I would not take something that is meant for them."

"Good," Gregory said. "That's Noble." He paused. "But it's blood. Fortified with vitamins and minerals. To sustain vampires."

Christopher sat very still. Processing.

"Most of the congregation," Gregory continued. "They are vampires. Notice, after a sermon, they don't chit-chat or gossip? They thank you. Shake your hand. Leave."

Christopher's eyes widened slightly.

"And their hands," Gregory said. "Always cold. Even during the summer."

"I..." Christopher started. Stopped. "I had noticed that."

"But the killing," Christopher said. "The draining of blood. All the things I have heard about vampires."

"Yes," Gregory said quietly. "They did do that. Out of desperation and starvation. The pantry is an alternative for them. To be fed and not starve."

Christopher was silent for a long moment. Then he spoke.

"If a wicked person turns away from all the sins they have committed and keeps all my decrees and does what is just and right, that person will surely live; they will not die." Christopher's voice was steady. "Ezekiel 18:21."

He looked at Gregory.

"I cannot condemn a person who comes before God and atones for his sins and wants to change their ways."

Gregory let out a breath he hadn't realised he was holding.

"They are in your hands now, Father," Gregory said. "Be kind. Be stern. Be just. For they deserve nothing less."

Christopher's brow furrowed. "What do you mean, in my hands?"

Gregory looked towards the church and said nothing more.

Christopher felt something cold settle in his chest. But he pressed on.

"Who else knows?" Christopher asked. "About the vampires?"

"Everyone," Gregory said simply. "Ted. Margaret knew. The other regulars in the parish. Phil. I believe Markus suspects, but it does not bother him."

"And the diocese?"

"They have no idea. As long as the Roman fort keeps money flowing towards them, they ignore the rest. The money we get from the vampire donations. It's enough to sustain us and help all the other parishes on the marsh that the diocese has ignored."

"I was speaking with the deacon of another marsh parish," Christopher said. "He mentioned a sudden influx of donations. Paid for a new roof. Heating system replaced."

"Yes," Gregory said. "Vampire donations, sent anonymously through the internet."

Christopher sat back. Absorbing it all.

"And what about the billionaire benefactor who visits us?" Christopher asked. "Who offers support to all of us. Is she...?"

"Yes," Gregory said. "She also runs a foundation that has been curing human blood-borne viruses for the last eighty years."

Christopher's head was spinning. The entire world reorienting.

They sat in silence for a moment. The roses. The bench. The quiet.

Then he looked at Gregory. Really looked. Saw the grey in his face. The way he sat hunched. The exhaustion.

"And what can the church do for you?"

Gregory was quiet for a moment. Then:

"Nothing can be done for me, for I am dying. The strain on my body from being mid-state is tearing it apart. And I don't have much longer."

The words landed heavily. Final.

Christopher's face went pale. "I do have to admit, now that you say it... since Margaret passed, you look like you've aged thirty years."

Gregory nodded. "I know."

"What can I do to help?" Christopher asked. His voice breaking.

"Be a good pastor to these people," Gregory said simply.

Silence settled between them. The roses moved slightly in the breeze.

"One last thing," Gregory said. "You will be asked sometimes to end someone's existence. This is a mercy."

Christopher looked at him sharply.

"Dr. Sarah will give you what you need and teach you. Or someone you trust to administer it."

Gregory stood slowly. Steadied himself.

"They are good people, Christopher. Lost. Suffering. Trying to find their way back."

He looked at the younger priest.

"Help them."

Christopher nodded. Unable to speak. Just nodded.

Gregory walked back towards the church. Each step is slower than it used to be.

Christopher sat alone on the bench in The Heirloom. The truth was settling over him like a weight.

The hush remained. Sacred. Waiting.

And somewhere in the roses, Margaret's voice seemed to whisper.

"Mind your step. We are resting here."

CHAPTER XXX – "The End"

"I am the Alpha and the Omega, the First and the Last, the Beginning and the End" - Revelation 22:13

Gregory lay on his bed.

Ted stood at one side. Umbra, Sarah, Phil, Markus, and Father Christopher close by. They spoke in low voices, then not at all.

Outside, the garden and the road beyond were full. Hundreds had come. Parishioners. Travelers. Vampires who had passed through once and were never forgotten.

No one spoke.

They stood in silence.

Gregory opened his eyes. Looked around the room. Smiled.

"Give the people what they want," he said quietly, "and you get a crowd."

Sarah shook her head. "Must you?" she said.

But she was smiling. Her eyes were wet.

Gregory looked at them all.

"I have lived more in these seventeen years than in all the rest of my life combined," he said. "And all of you made that possible."

A breath.

"For that, I am grateful."

Umbra said nothing. She had seen centuries pass. Empires rise and fall. She had stood at the end of more lives than she could count.

Still—she wiped at her eye.

"If Margaret were here," she said quietly, "she would have brought tissues. Red ones."

A few of them smiled.

Father Christopher stepped forward. His hands trembled.

"Shall I…?" he asked.

Gregory nodded.

"I'll send your regards to Carey," Gregory said to Umbra. "I expect he's organizing things already."

Umbra let out a breath that might have been a laugh.

Christopher began.

"Go forth, Christian soul, from this world, in the name of God the almighty Father, who created you…"

His voice steadied as he continued.

"The Lord is my shepherd; I shall not want…"

He paused. Looked at Gregory.

"Lord Jesus, holy and compassionate…"

His voice broke.

"…forgive Gregory…"

He stopped.

Tried again.

Couldn't.

"Father Gregory has no sins," he said, and the words dissolved into tears.

Gregory reached out. Took his arm.

Smiled.

Then his hand loosened.

And he was gone.

No one moved.

The room held its breath.

Outside, the silence remained.

A moment later, a thunderclap rolled across the sky.

Phil looked up sharply. "He wasn't an ancient…"

A jet passed overhead, fast and low,

the sound trailing behind it. Umbra watched it go.

A faint smile touched her lips.

"I thought he deserved a proper vampire sendoff,"

she said quietly.

Gregory lay in state in the church for three days.

They placed him at the front, where he had stood so many evenings before. Hands folded. Eyes closed. At rest.

Candles burned without interruption. Replaced as they guttered down. No one allowed the light to fail.

People came.

They moved quietly through the church. Some stayed only a moment. Others sat for hours. No one was turned away.

Humans. Vampires. Travelers who had passed through once and returned.

They stood before him. Sat in the pews. Said nothing.

Outside, the road was filled. The garden. The fields beyond.

Ted remained near the front. Seeing to small things that did not need seeing to.

Sarah came and went. Once, she stood beside Gregory for a long time, studying him. Then she stepped back.

Umbra stayed.

She stood near him, not touching. Watching.

She said nothing.

On the third day, the church was full again before dusk. The air had grown still.

Father Christopher stood near the altar. There was nothing left to say.

They remained.

Time passed.

Then—

A small movement.

Ted frowned.

Gregory's hand shifted.

Barely.

Ted stopped.

"Sarah," he said quietly.

She was already moving.

Another moment.

No one spoke.

Gregory's chest lifted.

Once.

Then again.

A sound moved through the room

caught before it became a voice.

Umbra did not move.

Gregory's eyes opened.

He stared upward for a moment. Unfocused.

Then slowly, he turned his head.

Saw them.

The room. The light. The faces.

Something in his expression changed. No surprise. Not confusion.

Recognition.

He was still for a moment longer.

Then, quietly:

"I guess I am no longer mid-tier."

A cry broke from the back of the church.

One of the tourists was visiting the Roman section.

Phil was there in an instant.

"It's all right," he said quietly. "Just a reflex."

He guided her toward the door. She didn't resist.

The door opened. Closed.

Psalm 136

*"Give thanks unto the Lord; for he is good: for his mercy
endureth for ever."*

This is a work of fiction. Names, characters, places, and
incidents either are the product of the author's imagination or are used
fictitiously. Any resemblance to actual persons, living or dead, events,
or locales is entirely coincidental.

ISBN: 9798995923312
LCCN: 2026907990

ACKNOWLEDGMENTS
The author would like to thank Terri Rioux for being the beta reader of
this story and providing excellent feedback.

DEDICATION
This book is dedicated to Linda Capel, who was the first person
to encourage me to write. It only took twenty years...

A NOTE ABOUT ROMNEY MARSH
*This story takes place among the fourteen medieval churches of
Romney Marsh - real sanctuaries that have stood for centuries. Each is
unique: Brookland's octagonal belltower, Fairfield across the marsh,
smugglers' murals at Snargate. They're living history, and they need
our care. Visit **romneymarshchurches.org.uk** for virtual tours, audio
guides, and visitor information, Walk where Gregory walked. See what
Margaret saw. History needs us to keep building.*

Find out more about the story and the author at vampirepriest.com